MW00718389

Perfect Timing

...a hotter than sin love story with Ms. Dare's trademark BDSM sprinkled in... I never want her stories to ever end, and Bi Now, Gay Later is no exception. The emotional storyline and the sexual heat kept me wanting more.
~ *Two Lips Reviews*

I rooted for these guys all the way through the story hoping for a HEA as only Kim Dare delivers. I love how her BDSM elements showcase the perfection of their relationship and its flaws. Jerry and Denton were wonderful and Bi Now, Gay Later is my favorite of the Perfect Timing series thus far.
~ *Fallen Angel Reviews*

Total-E-Bound Publishing books by Kim Dare:

Pack Discipline:
The Mark of an Alpha
The Strength of a Gamma
The Duty of a Beta

Perfect Timing:
You First
Silent Night
Time to Do
Bi Now, Gay Later

Collared:
Turquoise and Leather
Imperial Topaz

G-A-Y:
Gaydar
Gay Like You
Gay Until Graduation
Gay Since Today
Gay Pride
Gay Porn
Gay for Pay
Gay Divorcee

Anthologies:
Threefold: Trust, Love, Submit
Night of the Senses: Whispers
Caught in the Middle: Between Tooth and Paw
Friction: Yes!
Gaymes: Elliot's War

Seasonal Collections:
Christmas Spirits: The Gift
My Secret Valentine: Secret Service
Summer Seductions: In the Heat of the Moment

Mistletoe and Submission

PERFECT TIMING
Volume Three

Bi Now, Gay Later

The Stroke of Twelve

KIM DARE

Perfect Timing Volume Three
ISBN # 978-0-85715-411-8
©Copyright Kim Dare 2011
Cover Art by Natalie Winters ©Copyright 2011
Interior text design by Claire Siemaszkiewicz
Total-E-Bound Publishing

This is a work of fiction. All characters, places and events are from the author's imagination and should not be confused with fact. Any resemblance to persons, living or dead, events or places is purely coincidental.

All rights reserved. No part of this publication may be reproduced in any material form, whether by printing, photocopying, scanning or otherwise without the written permission of the publisher, Total-E-Bound Publishing.

Applications should be addressed in the first instance, in writing, to Total-E-Bound Publishing. Unauthorised or restricted acts in relation to this publication may result in civil proceedings and/or criminal prosecution.
The author and illustrator have asserted their respective rights under the Copyright Designs and Patents Acts 1988 (as amended) to be identified as the author of this book and illustrator of the artwork.

Published in 2011 by Total-E-Bound Publishing, Think Tank, Ruston Way, Lincoln, LN6 7FL, United Kingdom.

No part of this book may be reproduced, scanned, or distributed in any printed or electronic form without permission. Please do not participate in or encourage piracy of copyrighted materials in violation of the authors' rights. Purchase only authorised copies.

Total-E-Bound Publishing is an imprint of Total-E-Ntwined Limited.

If you purchased this book without a cover you should be aware that this book is stolen property. It was reported as "unsold and destroyed" to the publisher and neither the author nor the publisher has received any payment for this "stripped book".

Manufactured in the USA.

BI NOW, GAY LATER

Dedication

To accepting people for who they really are.

Chapter One

"Do you reckon he spends a lot of time thinking about having sex with women?"

Denton Greenwood's lips quirked into an amused little smile as he turned to his friend. "I have no idea who you're talking about. But, since we're in a gay bar, I'll go out on a limb and guess that no one in here spends a lot of time thinking about doing anything with a woman."

"Jerry's not gay though, is he?" Peter pointed out. "He's bi."

Denton's fingers tightened around his glass as his eyes automatically sought out a blond head of hair in the crowd. Someone stepped to one side. Jerry came into view. "He's not bi."

"He says he's bi." Peter drained his glass and put it clumsily on the little table between their leather arm chairs. "Do you think that means he thinks about screwing women as often as he thinks about screwing men?"

Denton clenched his jaw as he watched Jerry nod his agreement with whatever the man standing next to him was saying. "He's gay."

Peter shook his head. "He says he's bi. He should know."

"I am his master," Denton snapped. "I know which way my lover swings, and Jerry is as gay as any man in this bar."

Even on his eighth pint, Peter seemed to realise he'd hit a nerve. "How's it working out between...?" he trailed off.

Denton continued to watch his lover speaking to some of his friends, all of them other collared submissives, on the opposite side of the room.

"Everything's fine," he snapped. It didn't sound like it when he bit the words out like that, but it was the truth.

In the months since Jerry had come under his protection, the younger man had turned out to be a damn near perfect match for him.

"He seems to have come into his own since you gave him his permanent collar," Peter offered.

Denton nodded. That was true too. He'd never guessed that the stunning, if rather tentative, submissive who had first come to his attention would thrive so well under his rules and discipline, but Jerry had a way of wrapping rules around himself as if they were a comforting blanket, and taking every limitation his master put upon him as a gift. And, more than any of that, he had a way of throwing himself so wholeheartedly into his submission that the idea of letting him go had quickly become unthinkable.

As loath as Denton was to act soppy for anyone, even Jerry, he could just about admit that the submissive was the only one of his lovers he had ever actually fallen in love with. As long as they were alone and not doing anything overtly romantic at the time of any such admission, of course. A dominant had to hold on to some sort of standards. He wasn't so far gone that he was willing to shout it from the roof tops or let heart toting teddy bears worm their way into his life.

Denton held back a sigh. Damn near perfect, was all well and good. But knowing his lover could be *completely* perfect if he would just admit he was gay just made it all the more difficult to accept the younger man's stubborn insistence that he was bisexual with every day that passed. To feel perfection there, waiting just out of his reach, it was like a persistent itch at the back of Denton's neck.

Trying to push the issue out of his mind, the way he had so many times before, he ran his eyes down Jerry's body. It wasn't an easy task when so much of his lover's skin was concealed from him. For an absolutely gorgeous man, he was sweetly shy about his skin being put on display before anyone but his master. His inclination to hide himself away behind jeans and a long sleeve t-shirts whenever Denton hadn't made a point of ordering him into something different was damn near a fetish.

Right then Denton couldn't manage to smile indulgently at Jerry's bashfulness the way he usually did. Jerry was his—all of him, and he wasn't inclined to accept any part of his lover not being visible and available to him at that moment. He wasn't about to just sit around watching while Jerry's attention moved from one submissive to another and never once turned towards his master.

Rising from his chair, he left his friend sitting with the other dominants as he marched across the room. The moment he put his hand on Jerry's shoulder the younger man tensed. As he turned to face Denton, he realised exactly who was laying a hand on him and his expression morphed into a welcoming smile.

"May I serve you, master?"

"We're leaving. Is there anyone you need to say goodbye to?"

He saw Jerry cast a brief glance at the man he'd been speaking to. A silent understanding passed from one submissive to the other. Jerry shook his head. "No, master."

"Fetch our coats."

"Yes, master." Jerry turned and walked away through the crowd.

Denton watched him until he stepped out of sight before he turned his attention back to the man Jerry had been speaking to. He had something of the look of Jerry about him, the same blond hair and blue eyes, the same lightly muscled frame. He looked up and met Denton's eye, before looking quickly down again.

"You belong to Phillips." Denton cast around for a name. Phillips went through a hell of a lot of submissives in very quick succession. It made it bloody difficult to keep track. "It's Michael, right?"

"Yes, sir," the man said, after a tiny hesitation.

Denton raised an eyebrow, sure he'd managed to dredge up the right name.

"I'm still under his protection, sir, but Mr. Phillips is looking for a new master for me. He's decided that we do not suit well enough to make his arrangement with me a permanent one."

Denton caught Michael's eye as he risked another glance up. For all the submissive's carefully worded language, it was obviously a mutual decision. Denton had a vague memory of Peter saying something about them deciding to part ways because Michael wanted a more old fashioned style of mastery. Or maybe not. After a while all his friend's gossip blurred together.

Jerry came back to his side, holding their coats and neatly saving him from having to think of something suitable to say to Michael. Denton nodded his dismissal to Phillips' submissive. "Tell your master I send him my regards."

"Yes, sir," Michael said, smiling his goodbye to Jerry as he turned his attention to another of his friends standing nearby.

Denton took his coat from his submissive. By the time he shrugged his shoulders and felt his leather jacket settle comfortably around his body, he was already on his way out of the club. Jerry seemed taken off guard by his sudden departure. He was still pulling his smaller jacket on when he caught up with him at the door to the club.

If Phillips' lover had been anything other than a perfectly unobjectionable submissive, Denton knew he would have latched on to Jerry's conversation with him as an excuse. As it was, he gave no reason for the tight grip he took on his pet's wrist as they stepped into the night air.

Striding briskly across the car park, he only just shortened his stride enough to let Jerry's shorter legs keep pace with him. As they stopped by his car, Denton heard the change in his submissive's breathing as it sped up in anticipation. The younger man had obviously recognised his master's altered mood and what it meant. His pulse fluttered faster under Denton's grip around his wrist. He glanced up at his master, waiting for the first order, for the scene to start in earnest.

"Strip."

Denton let go of his wrist and stepped in front of him, shielding him from the sight of anyone else who might choose that moment to leave the club. Jerry didn't even glance towards the club door before he shrugged his jacket back off. All his attention was focused on his master. Knowing that soothed Denton's instinct to display his possession of his lover a fraction, but it wasn't near enough to quell it.

Jerry looked to him for further instruction. Denton held out a hand to receive the jacket. The moment his hands were free, Jerry reached for the hem of his long sleeve t-shirt. Pulling the thin material over his head, he folded it neatly and handed it over. Lowering himself to each knee in turn, his pet began to pull his boots and socks off.

Denton managed to look away from his lover for long enough to scan the rough concrete and check there was nothing on the ground that might cut his feet, but his focus reverted entirely to Jerry as the younger man gave up his footwear to his master. Without any sign of doubt or hesitation, Jerry's hand went to his fly. The black denim was soon pushed down, taking his boxers with them. He folded and surrendered them without comment.

As Denton studied him, a shiver ran through the younger man's body. If Denton was any judge, that had far more to do with nervous excitement than the cool air filling the car park. Jerry was already starting to harden very pleasingly for his master.

Opening the car door, Denton tossed his pet's clothes onto the back seat. Slamming the door again, he turned back to his lover and looked him over very slowly. A simple hand gesture ordered the submissive to turn around.

"Hands on the back of your head."

Jerry raised his hands and laced his fingers on the back of his head, presenting himself for a thorough inspection as he made another slow revolution in front of his master.

Only a tiny patch of Jerry's skin was hidden from him now, that little strip that lay under his collar. Denton tucked his fingers under the black leather and ran his knuckles all the way around Jerry's neck so no bit of him remained unexamined, untouched by his master's hands or eyes .

A door banged behind them. Men called to each other, laughing and yelling their goodbyes as they left the club. Jerry looked up and met Denton's eyes, making a point of not looking at the other men, of not trying to work out if he was exposed to them or not.

A sweet little blush crept to his cheeks, but his hands stayed on the back of his head while Denton kept his fingers tucked under his collar and held his gaze.

Somewhere at the other end of the car park, someone started a car and drove away. A minute later another car drove off. Denton kept Jerry standing there as silence filled the air once more, daring him to object, to look away, to do anything other than follow his master's orders.

He waited for any sign of weakness from his submissive, any hint of disobedience. He searched for any indication that Jerry didn't belong to him in every way one man could belong to another, that he didn't trust him to take complete and perfect care of any man under his protection.

"May I serve you, master?" Jerry asked softly, his eyes flickering here and there as he searched Denton's face for any indication of how he could please him.

A man couldn't find sign of disobedience where it didn't exist. Denton nodded, just once, allowing his submissive a tiny moment of praise before he opened the front passenger side door. "Get in. Keep your hands where they are."

Jerry got carefully into the seat, his hands still glued to his scalp. Denton slammed the car door and quickly strode around to his own side of the vehicle.

Sliding in behind the driver's seat he spared a quick glance at his submissive, debating the merits of letting Jerry move his hands to do up his seatbelt, over doing the job himself.

The question faded from his mind as the brief glance turned into a more detailed study. He looked his pet over very slowly, taking in every gorgeous detail.

It was always easier to smile at Jerry's persistent inclination towards modesty in public when they were alone, when he'd been stripped down to be admired in private. There was a part of him that loved knowing every bit of Jerry's body belonged to him and no one else, that no one else even got to look at him. But, for once, abstract knowledge of possession wasn't enough to satisfy him. As pretty as they were, displays of physical possession didn't feel like enough, either.

"Legs wider," he ordered, automatically correcting his lover's posture while he searched his mind for something, anything, that might fix the uncontrolled spiral of emotions whirling inside him.

Jerry spread his knees as far apart as he could while still allowing room for his master to change gears once they set off. Denton looked him over again. His pet had hardened further. His erection was starting to rise and curve back towards his stomach. Denton nodded to himself, pleased that Jerry was so quick to enjoy a scene that was far more to his master's taste than his own.

"Mouth open."

Jerry licked his lips and parted them slightly.

Fully exposed, fully accessible, offering himself freely to his master to do with as he pleased, he looked just as fantastic a submissive as Denton knew he was. It wasn't fair to treat him as if he was anything less than that, just because he was annoyed with a situation that was just as much his fault as Jerry's. If he wanted him to be perfect, it was his job as the master in their relationship to see that his pet came out of the closet properly.

Tucking a knuckle under his pet's chin, Denton guided him to turn to face his master. Although he was still hard, Jerry also seemed wary now, as if he knew something was wrong in his master's world, but couldn't work out what.

Leaning across the car, Denton brought their lips together. He'd intended it to be a quick moment of reassurance, just to let Jerry know that his master had realised what the problem was, and would see that it was fixed. That idea disintegrated the moment their mouths touched.

Denton slid his other hand into Jerry's hair, brushing his pet's hands away from the back of his head so he had free reign to tangle his own fingers in the thick, blond strands and tilt Jerry's head back so he could taste his parted lips properly.

There was no room for pretence. He took possession of the younger man's mouth, dragging a whimper out of him as Jerry instinctively acknowledged his master's ownership of him.

Denton tightened his grip, pulling Jerry forward until he knew his pet would realise his master no longer expected him to maintain the position he'd ordered him to assume less than a minute earlier. Jerry got the hint. He leaned into the kiss, offering everything to his master as easily and as instinctively as anyone ever could.

Even with need to possess and dominate pounding though him, part of Denton was still in control enough to study the scene as if from the outside looking in. That part of him which always tried to watch each scene from a distance so he could make the tough decisions objectively, nodded its head as it realised a tipping point had been reached.

Every bit of Jerry belonged to him. There could be no more doubts about that. There could be no more half measures or half labels. Complete perfection wasn't going to wait any longer.

Denton felt something click into place inside him. The uncomfortable feeling that had grown within him every time he heard the word bi began to ease. In hindsight, the sensible half of him could only conclude that it was a miracle that the other side of him, the side of him that wanted to own, to possess, to love without boundary or restraint, had managed to pretend that Jerry's insistence on the bi label was only a *mild* annoyance for so long.

Denton broke the kiss as suddenly as he'd initiated it. Pulling back, he stared down at his lover. The world inside his head might have changed, but his pet was the same as ever. Jerry blinked and stared up at him, his breaths coming in pants as he licked his lips and stole a final taste of his master's kiss.

Their gazes locked together and Jerry didn't seem to be able to look away. He looked so wide-eyed and dazed, so flawless. And he was flawless, Denton reminded himself. All Jerry had to do was finish coming out, and it would be official.

Minutes passed. Jerry dropped his gaze. His hands had been free to do as they pleased since Denton pushed them out of his hair. He reached out to his master and put his hand on his thigh, very close to the bulge of his erection behind the denim. "May I, master?"

The words hung in the air between them.

His first instinct was to say no, he wanted his pet back in their apartment. He wanted everything settled between them once and for all, and there was no way in hell he was going to play out that scene in his car.

Jerry's tongue flicked out to moisten his lips again. He hadn't lifted his gaze from his master's erection. Denton held back a moan at the sight of him so eager and ready to please.

For once, it was the sensible, objective part of him that put up its hand and voted for immediate sex. There was no point rushing home for a serious scene when his brain was settled so firmly below his belt. Trying to have that particular conversation when he couldn't focus on anything his lover said because he was too busy fantasising about all the other things his submissive could be doing with his mouth was a sure way to send the scene to hell.

It was far better to take care of his lust right there in the car park than to muddy the situation when they got back to the house. Coming was important, but having a clear head to take care of Jerry in the scene he had planned was vital. That realisation made the decision for him.

Denton nodded his permission. He was tall. The driver's seat was already pushed back almost as far as it would go. He adjusted the settings and let it slide back the last inch, giving Jerry as much room as he could.

His pet didn't waste any time. He reached for his master's belt the moment Denton straightened in his seat. A second later he had his fly undone. His hand slid past the tangle of material to guide his cock out from between the layers of cotton boxers and denim.

Pre-cum leaked from the tip. A dainty swipe of Jerry's tongue and his pet swallowed it down, murmuring his approval as he rubbed his lips back and forth over the head. Vibrations shot straight up Denton's spine. His hand moved to rest on the back of Jerry's neck. It lingered there for a while, enjoying the feel of the leather under his palm as Jerry's collar shifted with each movement of his throat.

His pet dipped his head further, taking the topmost inches of Denton's shaft into his mouth. Liquid heat surrounded the glans, quickly followed by delicious suction. Jerry's tongue swirled around the head, gathering up more pre-cum as it leaked into his mouth. He tilted his head to the side, letting Denton know that his pet remembered how much his master loved to see every detail.

The dominant stared down, watching his lover's lips thin into a pale pink line as he slid his mouth down his erection. The suction increased as Jerry pulled back, his tongue danced against Denton's cock as if his lover was more determined than ever to do anything and everything he could think of to offer his master pleasure.

No man in his right mind could watch the way Jerry went down on him and still believe his pet wasn't gay. Denton dropped his head back against the head-rest as his pet pulled a groan of pleasure from deep within him. He reluctantly let his eyes fall closed, eager to watch, but needing to make it last too.

A noise from outside the car made him open his eyes again and turn his attention to the view out of the windshield.

The club door swung open. Several men walked across the car park. If Jerry heard them, he gave no sign of it. Denton took a slow deep breath and tried to study the impromptu little scene objectively.

Jerry was bowed down out of sight of the other men, perhaps a few of them would wonder why he was just sitting there in the car park. One or two might even guess why Jerry wasn't in sight. But that wasn't important right then. Other men were irrelevant. There was no need to change anything.

Peter waved as he walked across to his car, faithfully steered by his own submissive, Benedict. The collared man offered Denton slight smile as he guided his drunken master into the passenger seat of their car before he got in to drive them home.

Denton stroked his fingertips up Jerry's bare back. His pet sucked harder around his shaft as he arched into the contact. Willing to indulge his lover's desire to feel his master's touch, to feel a *man's* touch, Denton repeated the action with the palm of his hand, stroking the skin down along the line of Jerry's spine until his fingers dipped between his lover's buttocks.

Jerry whimpered and scrambled to shift his position and move his legs further apart in offering. Out of Jerry's line of sight, Denton shook his head. It was bad enough feeling like a teenager who couldn't control his cock well enough to wait until he was out of the car park. There was no way in hell either part of him was going to agree to scramble around in the confined space trying to find a way for a man his height to top his lover properly.

"When we get home," he said, his voice rough with arousal. "If you're good and do as your master says, you might be allowed to come then."

Jerry moaned his approval around his cock. His efforts to please his master re-doubled. The hands resting on Denton's thighs to steady the submissive tightened their grip. He sucked hard and fast, his head bobbing over his lap more and more rapidly with each moment. Maybe he was in a rush to finish his master off so he could have his own turn, but it felt more like a simple need for a submissive to know he had pleased his master — for a gay man to know he had pleased his lover.

Denton tangled his fingers in Jerry's hair. His hips thrust forward. He buried himself deep in his lover's mouth as he came across his pet's tongue. Muscles worked rapidly around his cock as Jerry sucked and swallowed as fast as he could, never missing a drop.

His yell when he came seemed to echo in the close confines of the car. By the time the silence came back, Jerry's mood seemed to have changed. If there had been any inclination to rush before, all sign of it disappeared the moment the submissive tasted his master's pleasure.

He sucked slowly and gently around Denton shaft as it softened in his mouth. For a few minutes, Denton found his own rush to be back at their apartment and starting the important scene of the night wasn't so urgent either.

He stroked his fingers through the younger man's hair, absentmindedly smoothing down those locks that stood up at strange angles after he'd taken hold of it. He let a few more minutes pass in peaceful silence before he prompted Jerry to lift his head.

His lover let his shaft slip from between his lips with obvious reluctance and looked up at him. Denton slipped his fingers into the younger man's collar and pulled him close for a deep kiss.

There was a reason why the sensible part of him existed. Denton felt the taste of himself in his pet's mouth ease his desire to rush in and damn the consequences a fraction more. For the first time since they left the club, he truly felt sane enough to drive, sane enough to lead the scene properly when they got home.

He unhooked his fingers from Jerry's collar and nodded his approval.

"As you were."

Jerry immediately sat back in his seat and resumed the position his master had ordered him into when they first sat in the car. As the last little detail fell into place and Jerry let his lips fall apart in offering, Denton felt his control over the world around him come back into complete focus.

Tidying up his own clothes, he put on Jerry's seat belt before clicking his own into place. Practical considerations taken care of, he nodded once more. Decisions made. Brain back above belt. They were ready to tackle the important issues.

Putting the car into gear, he steered them out of the car park, trusting the tinted windows to take care of Jerry's inclination towards modesty on the journey home.

As they drove through practically deserted streets, his lover's breathing failed to settle into a proper relaxed rhythm. He seemed to be stuck on the edge, only needing a word to push him over, but lacking the permission he required before he could come. By the time Denton pulled into the car park under their building, Jerry's eyes were dropping closed as he began to completely lose himself in the depths of his submission.

Denton left him sitting in that same position as he got out of the car and walked around to the passenger side. Jerking the door open, he studied Jerry very carefully. He still hadn't moved a muscle.

"Move freely. Get out. Put your jeans on. Carry the rest."

It would be a million to one chance if they ran into someone on the short journey up to the fifth floor at this time of night. The jeans were concession enough to make. Given the emotions still pounding through him right then, Denton was quietly pleased with the objective side of himself for remembering that jeans should be considered necessary.

Taking his pet by the wrist the moment he'd done up his fly, Denton walked him barefoot across the car park. He slowed his pace just enough to scan the floor in front of them for anything that might cut an unshod foot, but that was still the only allowance he was capable of right then. His grip around Jerry's wrist remained firm until they stepped into their apartment.

When he finally let go of him, Jerry hesitated, suddenly looking a little lost and unsure of what was expected of him. A second later, he lowered himself to his knees at his master's feet. One glance and Denton knew that his lover still sensed something off in his mood.

An orgasm might have given him back a little of his control, but hadn't been enough to clear his need to get everything settled between them that night. Jerry obviously still sensed the tension running through his blood.

"I'm going to tie you up," Denton told him, automatically offering his submissive a piece of concrete information to centre himself on.

As easily as he said the words, Denton saw Jerry relax. "Yes, master."

"In the playroom. I want you naked and ready to stay in bondage for several hours by the time I enter the room. Offer your wrists and ankles to the central shackles. Leave your clothes here."

"Yes, master."

Jerry removed his jeans and went quickly into the playroom that had been created out of the apartment's second bedroom. He left the door ajar behind him the way Denton's rules demanded, as if it no longer even occurred to him that he could ever be closed in there without his master.

Seeing his willingness to obey every rule he'd ever set for the younger man once more eased Denton's rush to start the game immediately, or at least made him remember that Jerry's submission was too precious to be dealt with hastily. Forcing himself to be patient, he made a conscious effort to bring his emotions even further under his control before he walked into the scene.

Pacing across to the window, he looked down over the street outside. It was late and quiet. Not a thing moved. There was nothing to distract him from his desire to have the issued settled once and for all.

Denton took a deep breath. Tonight had been a long time in coming, but it was definitely time. That was one thing that every warring side of his personality could agree on. His reaction to Peter's casual mention of the subject was all the proof he need. Anything that made him feel so out of control couldn't be tolerated. It wasn't fair to either of them. Jerry deserved a master who was in control of every aspect of their lives.

He looked across to the playroom door as he considered the scene ahead of them. All sounds of Jerry moving about within the room had already ceased. Denton had seen him under the shackles often enough to know the picture he would present. Standing in the middle of the room, wrists touching the outer edge of the padded leather restraints hanging from the ceiling, ankles likewise touching those bolted to the floor at his feet. His pet would wait there, bound by nothing more than his master's command, for as long as Denton demanded—his body and his submission laid out for his master to view at his convenience.

Denton let him wait a little while longer, while he ran the scene he wanted to conduct over and over inside his head, looking for things that might go wrong. It was essential that he be able to deal with any problem that might arise in the scene calmly and efficiently, without any hint of weakness—perhaps more so on this occasion than ever before.

It was a master's responsibility to look after his submissive. He couldn't let the scene hurt his pet. But Denton reminded himself it was also his responsibility to challenge the man under his protection, to encourage him to grow and to make progress in his submission as well as within his life in general, to help him be as perfect as he could be.

That's what he was doing, Denton repeated to himself. He was helping Jerry to take a leap forward. He was acting exactly as a good master should. He was doing this for Jerry. His own feelings on this particular topic had to become irrelevant now that the scene was going to start in earnest. It could only be about being a good master to the man he loved.

Denton nodded to the view out the window. It was time.

Chapter Two

Jerry Clarke took a deep breath and let it out very slowly, forcing his body to bring itself back under his conscious control as he stood in the centre of the playroom and waited for his master to bind him to the cuffs.

His master would be there soon, the worry inside him would settle and he would feel safe in his submission again. He knew that. It always happened that way. Knowing it didn't make it any easier to stand there and wait. His teeth worried his bottom lip as his eyes fell closed.

Nothing was wrong.

He hadn't done anything wrong. His master wanted to play, not punish. He hadn't done anything that would warrant a punishment, and his master was always scrupulously fair about such things. The same line of thought ran around and around inside his head, looping in circles, but it didn't change the fact that his master's mood wasn't one of those he was familiar with.

Something was wrong.

The playroom door closed with a click. Jerry's eyes sprang open. He stared across at his master. Denton wore the same serious expression that had lingered around his eyes since he'd announced they were going to leave the club.

He walked across to him without a word and stood close in front of him as he buckled the cuffs around his wrists and his ankles. His master's clothes brushed against Jerry's naked body, tempting him to hope for real contact, but the moment the restraints were in place, Denton stepped back.

"Submission isn't always easy," his master announced.

Jerry lowered his gaze, not sure what to say in response.

Denton threaded his fingers through his hair and tugged gently, making him look up. It was such a familiar touch, such a familiar action, it calmed Jerry's worries a little.

When Denton's hand was buried in his hair, it was easy to let his mind slip back to the car park when his head was bent over his master's lap and he knew exactly what his master expected of him and exactly how he could please the older man. He licked his lips and swallowed down the lingering taste of his master's pleasure.

Everything was fine.

"You understand that it is your master's place to make sure that you make progress as a submissive and as a man?"

"Yes, master," Jerry whispered.

Denton stared down at him for a long time.

Jerry cleared his throat as nerves built inside him all over again. "If I've done something that has displeased you, master—"

The dominant cut him off with a shake of his head.

Jerry stared up at the taller man, pushing the scene in the car out of his head as he tried to read what his master wanted from him now. "I can learn to be different, if I—"

Denton smiled slightly and stroked his cheek with the back of his knuckles while his other hand remained firmly tangled in his hair. "You don't need to be different. I am very pleased with you, just as you are. But it is well past time you faced certain facts about yourself."

Jerry frowned, annoyed with himself for not being able to understand. "Master?"

Denton's hand dropped from his cheek to his collar and trailed along the line of the leather. For one horrible moment, Jerry imagined his master would take the mark away. It was a groundless sort of panic, but that didn't make it any easier to push the sudden rush of emotion aside. He swallowed again, just to feel the reassuring movement of leather around his throat, reminding him who he belonged to.

His master's hand trailed lower, caressing his skin along his collarbone before stroking back up his neck to touch his face. Leaning into his master's touch the way he always did, Jerry stared up at him and once more tried to work out what was going on. A frown creased between Denton's dark brows, but he seemed to be deep in thought rather than genuinely displeased with his pet.

Jerry swallowed again as his master stared back at him. "Master?" he asked.

Denton's lips twitched into a smile. "You're a fantastic submissive."

Jerry offered him a tentative smile at the unexpected compliment.

"But a tendency towards submission can make a man somewhat less than certain about some parts of his life."

Until that evening, Jerry had been pretty damn sure he was certain about every part of his life. Since he'd come under his master's protection, his life had been all about that concrete sort of certainty that he loved. "I'm sure I want to belong to you, master," he offered.

A smile flickered over Denton's lips again. "I've never doubted that. This isn't about me."

Jerry looked down, sure that he should understand what his master wanted from him, but unable to follow the older man's thoughts.

"How long has it been since you had sex with a woman?"

That made Jerry raise his gaze for a moment, but he quickly looked away. His master knew the answer full well. "Three years, master."

"And have you missed having sex with women in those three years?" Denton asked, his hand stroking down his neck and along his collar bone again.

Jerry shook his head as the skin under Denton's touch began to tingle with pleasure at being the focus of so much unexpected attention.

"Real answers," his master ordered.

"No, master, I haven't." For a large part of that time he'd belonged to Denton. "I haven't missed having sex with other men ei—"

Denton touched his lips, silencing him as effectively with one fingertip as anyone else could with their whole hand, easily stopping him from saying that he didn't miss having sex with *anyone* but his master.

"We're not talking about how you think about men," Denton corrected. "We are speaking, specifically, about how you may or may not feel about women." He took his fingertip away and trailed it down Jerry's body until it brushed across his nipple.

Jerry bit his lip, not sure if he was allowed to respond to his master's touch freely in the middle of this sort of conversation.

"You like a man's touch, don't you?" Denton asked.

Jerry nodded. "Yes, master."

"More than a woman's touch?" He dropped his hand further to brush the back of his knuckles up and down his stomach, teasing his abs until they twitched under the all too gentle caress, making him sway within his bondage.

Jerry shook his head. "I...I like my master's touch more than anyone else's."

"More than you would like a mistress's touch?" Denton pushed.

Jerry looked down his body and watched Denton's hand tease his skin. "I don't want anyone but you touching me, master."

"Answer the question," Denton said, a sudden snap lending force to the order.

Jerry closed his eyes. "I like a woman's touch just as much as a man's touch, master," he admitted, since it was obviously what his master was trying to get him to say.

"You've been telling yourself that for a long time, haven't you?"

"Master?"

Denton smiled at him, but the smile didn't quite reach his eyes. "You're not the first man to use the label as a stepping stone on your way out of the closet, Jerry. But it's time to take the final step now."

"I don't understand," Jerry said, although he had a horrible feeling that he knew exactly what was coming next.

"It's time for you to accept that you're gay," Denton announced.

"I'm bi, master," Jerry whispered.

The half smile disappeared. Denton's eyes turned very serious. "No, you're not."

"Master, I..." Jerry trailed off, not sure what words might help the situation and what might make it worse.

"I'm not denying that this whole situation is partially my fault for having humoured you for so long," Denton told him. "Perhaps if I'd made you face facts earlier, this would be easier for you. But either way, it's time you accepted the truth properly."

Jerry dropped his gaze and watched his master's hand as it moved lower again and wrapped around his aching erection.

"Master..."

Denton began to flex his fingers around his shaft, not jacking him off, but making it very hard to ignore the fact his master literally held him in the palm of his hand. "You're gay."

Jerry shook his head.

"You like men. You find men, desirable, sexually attractive." His thumb stroked back and forth across the tip of Jerry's cock, spreading the pre-cum over the head.

"I..."

"You find me attractive," Denton added, as he began to slowly stroke him, smearing the pre-cum down as shaft and making full use of all he had learnt about his lover's responses over the years. He knew what being jacked off in that slow calculating way did to him. After the blow job in the car, he had to know that it wouldn't take much to push him over the edge.

Jerry gasped and tried to make words happen. "Yes, master," he finally managed to bite out.

"There's nothing wrong with liking men, pet," Denton whispered in his ear.

He stepped closer to him, offering his shoulder for Jerry to rest his head on as he spoke softly to him, the way he only ever spoke in private. Jerry leaned into him, taking strength from the approval and comfort his master offered him. Each breath his master took made the muscles in his shoulder shift under Jerry's forehead. The easy rhythm soothed him just a fraction.

"It's nothing to be ashamed of," Denton said.

"I'm not ashamed, master," Jerry whispered back.

"Good boy," Denton praised, speeding up his strokes along the length of his shaft as reward.

"I'm not ashamed of liking women either, master," some foolishly honest part of Jerry forced him to add.

His master stepped back, taking away the supporting shoulder and the caressing hand.

"How often do you think about having sex with a woman?" he asked, his tone cooling with each word.

Jerry swayed in his restraints, pulling at them as he instinctively tried to regain his master's touch and follow him across the room. Denton didn't seem to notice that as he retreated to lean against the wall opposite him.

"I don't think about that," Jerry said. "I think about my master."

"Don't you think a genuinely bi-sexual man, if such a person should ever exist, would think about women more often?"

Jerry frowned. He knew it was the height of stupidity to mention a previous owner to a current one, but there seemed to be no way to avoid it. "When I belonged to Miss Stephens, I..."

Denton pushed himself away from the wall and strode around him. Jerry tried to turn his head to follow his master's progress, his words trailing off as he felt the anger pouring off the older man.

"I don't think about anyone other than you, master," he said again.

"You're gay," Denton stated.

Jerry said nothing. As Denton paced around behind him, he stared across the room at the empty white wall opposite him.

"There is no such thing as bisexuality."

Jerry picked a random point on the painted surface and fixed his gaze on it, as he tried his best not to listen—just as he always did when his master spoke on that particular subject. Denton saying it didn't make it true. Denton saying it didn't really mean anything at all.

His master loved him. Jerry knew that. Denton told him that, out loud and far more often than came easily to a man of his temperament.

His master loved him. Just because Denton didn't understand one part of him, that didn't mean he didn't love the rest of him. Jerry bit his lip and focused on that knowledge, doing his best to ignore his lover's words as they turned harsher and more dismissive of his sexuality by the moment.

Denton stopped in front of him. Jerry imagined that he could still see the same spot he'd been staring at on the wall. He did everything in his power to look through his master, to focus on a point in time and space that existed beyond this conversation.

The older man seemed to know what he was trying to do. He made him look up and look him in the eye instead. The hand in his hair failed to offer any comfort right then. While Denton demanded he hold his gaze, he had no choice but to focus on his master and take in every word he said.

"I've been very patient with you, Jerry. But the time has come for you to get out of the closet and make a real commitment to who you really are."

Jerry shook his head, not so much in answer as trying to deny this was happening, that his master could say all the words that echoed around inside his head.

"There is no such thing as bisexuality. It's time you faced up to that and stopped pretending otherwise. I'm sure it was easier when you first came out, but you don't need the crutch any more. You're gay."

Jerry closed his eyes. "Please, stop saying that," he whispered.

"It's the truth," Denton snapped. His hand ran down Jerry's body. For the first time, Jerry hesitated before he finally leaned into the touch, accepting it and welcoming it the way he knew a good submissive should.

Coming face to face with this side of his master's personality had softened him, but not so much that it took Denton more than a dozen strokes with a firm grip to have him aching to come all over again. His body found it far easier to ignore his master's words than his mind did.

"You like a man's touch," Denton whispered in his ear. He kept Jerry's cock in his fist, he kept up the strokes, as he moved around behind him. "You like the feel of a man's body against yours."

Jerry nodded when Denton pressed his body against his back, letting him feel his renewed erection through the material that separated them. His master still wanted him. Whatever he said, Denton wanted him. That was the important thing. "Yes, master."

"You like the feel of a man inside you too, don't you Jerry?"

Jerry pushed back against his master's fingers as they trailed down the cleft between his buttocks, teasing him with possibilities.

"You like the feel of your master's cock in your arse."

Jerry nodded.

His master's fingers disappeared for a second and came back coated in lube. Jerry murmured his pleasure as his master stroked his fingers around his hole. His whimpers quickly turned frustrated when they failed to enter him.

"Please, master?" Jerry whispered.

Denton slipped two fingers inside and immediately sought out his prostate. As one hand worked his cock and the fingers of the other hand thrust deeper inside him, all Jerry could do was hang from the chains and accept it all, enjoying every burst of pleasure that fired through him.

Each touch, each kiss his master applied to his neck wiped away some of the words his master had said. He just didn't understand, that was all. And dominants often had a tendency to be harsh when they dismissed those things that confused them. His master was a good man who loved him. A good submissive should be able to look past a few hurtful comments made by someone who couldn't possibly know how heartbreaking they could be for a man in his position.

Jerry caught up every ounce of submission inside him and held it tight, clinging to anything that might help him forgive his lover. It was practically impossible to think properly while Denton was still teasing him, but he somehow felt a little of his disappointment in his master drain away.

Groaning his approval of his touch if not his earlier words, Jerry tried to move between his master's hands, but no longer able to decide if he wanted to push back against one hand or thrust forward into the other.

"Do you like that, pet?" Denton asked him.

"Yes, master," Jerry murmured.

"Louder." Both his master's hands worked him faster, his right hand tightened around his shaft.

"Yes!" Jerry said. The half shout echoed around the room as Denton pushed him to the edge but refused that little bit of stimulation that would let him topple over into real pleasure.

"Do you want to come?"

"Yes!" It came out as another yell. Whimpering, trying to get himself back under control, Jerry tried again. "Yes, master," he rasped. "If it pleases you to let me come, I..."

Denton pressed another kiss to his neck. "It pleases me a great deal. You just have to do one thing for me."

Jerry nodded quickly, as ready as he ever was to do anything his master wanted, especially eager right then, to do anything that could bridge the gap Denton's words risked causing between them.

"All you have to do is say you're gay," Denton said.

Jerry blinked and tried to make his mind process the order. "Master?"

"Three little words and you can have whatever you want," Denton whispered in his ear. "All you have to say is, I...am...gay..." With each word, the fingers inside him rubbed against his prostate, tempting him to give in and just answer automatically.

Jerry shook his head.

"Jerry," Denton prompted.

"Can't."

"Yes, you can, Jerry. You're stronger than you think you are."

Jerry shook his head. It wasn't a question of strength, just honesty, and he couldn't lie to his master, not about something that important. "I can't."

35

"Yes, you can. Now, say the words for your master."

Jerry closed his eyes as tight as he could, trying to block out the idea he was failing Denton with his silence.

"If you say the words you can come," Denton coaxed as his hand moved over his erection again. He kissed his ear. "You can come in my mouth," he offered.

As simply as he said the words, Jerry's head was filled with the idea of Denton taking him in between his lips. For all his dominance and preference for topping, when he was in the mood, he gave head better than anyone Jerry had ever known.

Rough, demanding lips could turn into molten velvet when Denton wanted them to. Jerry whimpered and strained against his bonds as he imagined those lips wrapping around his cock, as he imagined his master's tongue running over his shaft as he suckled around the head.

"You can come in my arse," Denton whispered. "Would you like that, pet, would you like to top your master? Say the words for me and you can. Three little words and I'll give you anything you want."

Images swirled in his mind of Denton letting that happen for the first time. Jerry moaned as Denton held him on the edge and tempted him to jump and damn the consequences.

A huge part of him wanted to lie. His master would be happy with him if he lied. But when he parted his lips he knew what words were going to come out. "I'm bi, master."

Every muscle in Denton's body tensed. His hands stilled. He stepped away from Jerry, leaving him hanging alone and naked in the middle of the room as he slowly walked around to face him.

"You won't come until you learn to be honest," Denton informed him.

Jerry hung his head, feeling ashamed of who he was for the first time in so many years. Right then, as hard and as aching as he was, he couldn't make himself care about coming. All he wanted was for his master to cross the room to him and accept him, to hold him close and tell him that he was safe with the man who loved him. "Master?"

He somehow found the strength to lift his head and look his master in the eye. Denton knew what he wanted. His master had always been able to read what he needed in his expression, but he made no move to come closer to him, to reassure him.

"When you're ready to say the words," he told him.

Jerry dropped his gaze as he realised that they weren't just talking about an orgasm anymore. His master had no intention of truly accepting him in any way, shape or form, not until he said he was gay.

When he heard his master step forward, he thought he might have read him wrongly, that his panic had got the better of him the way he knew it sometimes did. He looked up at his master as Denton came within an inch of him. Their lips almost touched. Then he saw the look in his master's eyes.

The kiss would come as a reward when he said what his master wanted him to say. When he became the man his master wanted him to be. Jerry closed his eyes and took a deep breath, knowing there was only one option left open to him.

"Alcatraz."

Chapter Three

Denton stared down at his submissive. It took a full minute for the word to sink in to his mind and register as Jerry's safe word.

He took a step back, trying to find some mental space. A second later, he cleared his throat, trying to pull himself out of the scene and pull the objective side of himself to the surface so he could deal with the word properly.

"Did you cramp up?" he asked, looking up and down his submissive's body for any hint of a problem serious enough to make Jerry panic and invoke his safe word.

Jerry shook his head.

"Then what's wrong with you?" As much as he wanted to speak softly and tenderly to him, as much as he wanted to show the younger man that he knew how much courage it had taken for him to say his safe word, anger at Jerry's persistence was still pounding through him. The sensible side of him lost the battle. The words came out far more harshly than he intended.

Jerry flinched.

The movement was enough to remind him why such moments required patience and gentleness no matter how he felt within himself. Denton stepped forward and reached out to touch his pet's cheek, hoping to gentle him down enough that he could tell him what was wrong. Jerry jerked his head away from his hand.

"You told me that if I ever said my safe word, you'd stop, you'd let me go."

"Yes," Denton agreed.

Jerry's throat muscles worked rapidly as he swallowed several times. "I said my safe word."

Denton stared down at him, still trying to work out what was going on. "Jerry?" Stepping closer again, he stroked his fingers through his lover's hair. Jerry tried to pull away from his touch, but there was only so far he could go in his restraints.

Frowning, Denton touched his cheek again, signalling that his master wanted him to look up so he could look him in the eye. Jerry stopped fighting against his master's instructions, but he didn't look up, he just seemed to go limp within his restraints.

"Jerry?"

Jerry stared straight ahead as if he didn't even see his master standing in front of him.

"Jerry?" Denton prompted again.

"Please, wear a condom."

"What?"

"We both know that even if I wasn't bound, I'm still no match for you. All I've ever been able to do is say my safe word and hope that you'll respect it. If you're not going to stop when I ask you to, then I'm asking you to wear a condom when you…when do whatever it is you intend to do next."

Denton snatched his hand away from his lover as if Jerry's skin had turned into hot coals under his hand. "I have *never* done anything to make you say that."

Jerry closed his eyes. "I said my safe word," he repeated.

Yes, he had. Denton looked at the cuffs still wrapped firmly around his lover's wrist. In a moment, the leather was gone. Denton crouched down and undid the restraints at his ankles. As soon as he was free, Jerry stumbled away. His retreat only stopped when his back hit the wall.

Denton stood in the middle of the room, watching his every move, trying to work out what the hell was going on.

"I'm sorry, master," Jerry whispered. "I have to go now."

"What?"

Jerry looked to the door, then back to him. Caught between moving to block his escape route and stepping aside to give his lover the freedom to do what he wanted, Denton stayed where he was by the cuffs.

"I have to go now," Jerry repeated, seemingly as much to himself as his master.

"Where?"

"Somewhere that isn't here," Jerry said.

He'd wrapped his arms tight around his body, as if he was trying to comfort himself. He held himself close the way Denton had been more than ready to hold him, before all that bull about him being about to force Jerry fell from the sky.

"You're not making any sense, pet," Denton said, trying his best to make sure there was one man in the room who didn't sound like he was panicking. A pet might panic, a master couldn't.

"Please don't call me that," Jerry said. He lifted his hand to his collar and traced the leather, the way he so often did when he was nervous. Then his hand dropped away from the mark. "You should take this back."

"No!" Denton hadn't meant to shout, hadn't meant to make Jerry jump and press himself back against the wall, but the word echoed around the room, pushing Jerry even further away from him.

His lover closed his eyes. "Please, don't make me take it off myself. If I don't have any other choice I will, but please just…"

Denton stepped forward. "Jerry, you need to try and stay calm for me. If you tell your master what's wrong, I can help you, but you have to talk to me so I can do that. Understand?"

Jerry shook his head. "I have to go," he whispered. "You have to take the collar back and I have to go."

"Why?"

Jerry looked down. "I have to," he said again. "I…I can't wear this anymore."

He ran his fingers around the leather, looking for the buckle that would free it from his neck. His fingers scraped against his throat, scratching his skin as he scrabbled at the leather.

Denton didn't think. Objectivity went out the window. He stepped forward and took hold of Jerry's wrists before the younger man could hurt himself. Jerry gasped and flinched away as if he thought Denton would strike him.

Gentling his grip, Denton let go of Jerry's wrists. "I have no interest in hurting you. But if you pull at your collar like that, you are going to hurt yourself. I can't let that happen."

Jerry looked up at him. Their eyes met. Desperation swirled in the deep blue eyes. "Please, take it off," he begged.

Denton stared down at him. No matter how much the idea of taking the collar away turned his stomach, he couldn't refuse him right then. Everything else aside, Jerry had said his safe word. Denton knew he didn't have the right to refuse him whatever he asked for. He undid the buckle and took the collar away, hoping to earn a little of his lover's trust back, hoping Jerry would calm down enough to talk rationally and that would let them get the collar back on him as quickly as possible.

"Thank you," Jerry whispered. He seemed to bite back the honorific that naturally wanted to slip into the sentence. Denton's hand tightened around the collar in his hand as he realised Jerry wasn't calling him his master because right then he wasn't his master. The realisation made it impossible to think calmly and logically about anything.

The younger man looked past Denton to the door. "I have to go now."

"Where?" he asked, for what felt like the millionth time.

"I don't know," Jerry whispered. A frown gathered between his eyebrows as he said it, as if it really hadn't occurred to him that he needed to choose a destination.

"Don't you think you need to decide where you're going before you leave?" Denton asked, as gently as he could, hating himself for not being able to keep his impatience out of his voice entirely.

Jerry looked to the door again. He shook his head, dismissing that idea, as if Denton was the one who wasn't making any sense. Denton reached out to push the younger man's hair back from his face without even thinking about the familiar little gesture. Jerry flinched away from him again.

Denton lowered his hand. Jerry stepped around him, heading for the door. Unable to touch him and see that expression in his eyes again, Denton had no choice but to let him walk past him and out of the playroom.

Any slight hope that moving to a different room would break Jerry's panic disappeared as Jerry turned immediately towards the front door.

That snapped Denton into action. "Jerry!"

He hesitated, looking warily over his shoulder. "I have to…"

"You can't go anywhere stark bollock naked!"

Jerry looked down at his exposed body. "I haven't got any clothes," he said to himself. He cleared his throat. "Could I borrow some, please? I'll…I'll pay you for them as soon as I get a job."

"Jerry, you have a whole wardrobe full of clothes," Denton reminded him, struggling to keep anything like tolerance in his tone while his lover seemed to become less and less rational about everything by the minute.

Jerry shook his head. "They all belong to you. The same way I used to belong to you. They aren't mine."

"They're all four sizes too small for me. They're yours, you know that."

Jerry looked towards the bedroom they'd shared ever since he'd moved into his master's home. His gaze fell on the clothes he'd been wearing that night, where Denton had tossed them in the general direction of the chair in the corner.

"If I could just borrow them until I —"

"Put them on," Denton ordered.

Jerry quickly pulled his clothes on and headed for the door again.

"Jerry?" Denton called after him, not able to do more than that while every move he made towards his submissive made him panic even more.

For a moment, the younger man stopped with his hand on the door handle. "I'm sorry," he whispered. A moment later the door was closed behind him and he was gone.

Denton raced across to the window, grabbing his mobile phone off the hallway table as he went. By the time he stared down into the street below, he'd hit speed dial and the phone was ringing.

He didn't wait for the man on the other end to speak before he started issuing orders.

Jerry stood on the pavement outside his former master's apartment building. He looked both ways along the deserted street and bit his lip as he tried to work out what the hell he was supposed to do now. He wrapped his arms tight around his body, wondering if it was actually as cold as it felt or if he was going into some sort of shock. A shiver ran through him. His hands wouldn't stop shaking.

Turning, he looked up the lines of windows that filled the side of the building, but he stopped short of his master's window. It was stupid to think that his master…that his former master…would be there watching him. Jerry closed his eyes. Denton was probably glad to be rid of him. All things considered, he couldn't blame him.

He had to go somewhere further away from his master. Standing there on the pavement, being so close to him, that would only tempt him to run back into the building and beg the other man to take him back. Right then, it felt like it would be worth any price, any lie, if it meant he could have that collar back around his throat, if it meant he was allowed to belong to his master again.

No. That couldn't happen. Jerry repeated that fact to himself several times. There were things that were far more important than getting what he wanted. Some prices were too high.

Things were as they were now. They couldn't go back to the way they were before. He had to go to...to a homeless shelter, he guessed. He was homeless after all, without the security of a master or mistress for the first time in his adult life. Jerry stared at the crack in the paving stones under his feet and tried to remember the names of some of those charity buckets he'd thrown coins in over the years.

A car came around the corner. Jerry stepped back closer to the building, not wanting to draw attention to himself. The car stopped alongside him. Jerry ignored it, hoping whoever was driving it would ignore him too. It wasn't as if they lived in the middle of a red light district. There was no reason to think that any man stopping alongside him wanted anything more than directions from him. The panic boiling though his blood still made it impossible to really believe that right then.

Jerry closed his eyes. If the guy in the car wanted more than that, then it might pay for a bed for the night if he could find his way to a cheap hotel after the guy was done with him. His eyes scrunched closed even tighter.

The car door opened.

Someone stepped out.

Jerry forced himself to look up.

Peter Vickery, his master's friend, stood on the pavement in front of him.

"My master is—" Jerry cut himself off, unable to hold back a flinch at the out of date honorific. "Mr. Greenwood is upstairs, sir."

"And what are you doing out here?"

"I don't belong to him anymore, sir," Jerry whispered.

"Do you want to stay with us?" Mr. Vickery asked, not showing the slightest surprise at the announcement, possibly because he didn't sound incredibly sober.

Jerry shook his head.

"Benedict's in the car. You're welcome to use the guest room until you work out what you're going to do next."

Jerry looked from him to the car and back again. Benedict, Mr. Vickery's submissive, sat behind the wheel. He smiled encouragingly when he caught Jerry's eye.

"You know Benedict would have my balls on a platter if I laid a hand on another submissive," Mr. Vickery said with a rueful smile. "I'm just offering you the room, I'm not asking for anything from you in return."

Jerry swallowed, looking at the familiar face in front of him before turning his attention back to the deserted street. "I can work for my keep, sir."

Mr. Vickery nodded his acceptance, as if he never doubted it, and stepped back to guide him in to the car.

"You're not going to visit my...Mr. Greenwood?" Jerry asked as Benedict pulled away from the kerb and drove past the entrance to the visitor's car park attached to the block of apartments.

Mr. Vickery seemed to hesitate. "No, there wasn't anything important. We were just...uh...driving past and I thought we would..." he cleared his throat. "Are you hungry?"

Jerry shook his head, thinking he would be doing well if he made it to Mr. Vickery's house before he threw up. "No, thank you, sir."

When they got to the house, Mr. Vickery disappeared into his study to make a phone call, leaving Benedict to show him into the guest room.

"There's an en-suite through there and there's spare blankets on the shelf in the wardrobe. Do you want to borrow some pyjamas? We're about the same size. I've got a spare pair I've never worn."

Jerry looked down at his clothes, at the clothes that his master had bought for him. He ran his fingers along the edge of the shirt. "I'm fine in these, thank you."

Benedict hovered just inside the doorway.

"Thank you for letting me stay here tonight. If...I can find somewhere else tomorrow if..."

Benedict shook his head. "Don't be daft, you can stay here for as long as you want—until you and your master sort out things."

Jerry stared at the carpet. "Things aren't going to be sorted out," he whispered.

"Maybe..." Benedict began.

Jerry shook his head. "What's that thing they say— permanent and irreconcilable differences? I don't belong to Mr. Greenwood anymore. He took his collar back, and I left and...and I don't belong to him anymore."

* * * *

"He must have said something!"

Denton stood up and began to pace around his friend's living room. Peter and Benedict watched him go back and forth. He saw them exchange a glance.

"He must have told you what this is all about," Denton accused, swinging around to Benedict.

The submissive looked to his master for guidance.

"If Jerry's given you any explanation for his...for his breakdown, you should tell his master," Peter said.

"He says Mr. Greenwood's not his master anymore," Benedict pointed out.

Denton clenched his teeth and fought to be polite and rational about it all. The man had information. Venting his temper wasn't anywhere near as important as finding out what that information was.

Benedict saw his expression and seemed to realise he'd made a tactical error. He cleared his throat. "He hasn't said much, sir. And I've never been able to make much sense out of the things he does blurt out sometimes. He said that he didn't handle the situation very well, that he panicked."

Denton nodded for him to continue and tell him something he didn't know already.

"He said that a man like him couldn't belong to a man like you anymore." The submissive gave a frustrated sigh. "Practically the only thing I know for sure is that it all has something to do with him being bi."

Bi, gay or straight be damned. The only things that were important now were those things that would help him get Jerry back with his master where he belonged. Anything else could be sorted out later. Every part of the dominant agreed with that.

"Practically," Denton said, latching onto the word. "There's something else?"

Benedict looked to his master again and received a nod to continue. "He's still in love with you, sir."

"He said that?" Denton demanded, for once not caring if the other two men saw how desperate he was for that to be true.

Benedict gave one nod. "I don't think he meant to say it, it just sort of slipped out."

"You still don't know what went wrong?" Peter asked.

Denton collapsed back into one of the arm chairs opposite the sofa his friend sat on. "We were doing a scene and he just freaked out." He frowned, running the scene over in his mind for what felt like the millionth time. "I was pushing him hard, taking him out of his comfort zone. But I didn't touch on any of his hard limits. None that he'd ever told me about anyway..."

He took a deep breath. He'd known that challenging his pet that on the label he was so attached to would be difficult for him, but it didn't feel as simple as that when he looked back on the night. Jerry hadn't been angry, he hadn't been resistant or stubborn. It seemed to go far deeper than that, but his own memories were so clouded with his own emotions, it was hard to be sure about anything. He'd been ready to have that conversation with Jerry, yeah, right...

"He didn't have a mark on him," Benedict observed.

"And you know that how?" Denton demanded, eyes narrowing as he glared at the submissive.

"Because I made sure I accidentally walked in on him in the shower, sir," Benedict said, perfectly calmly. "He ran away from his master. He looked so terrified, like he was in so much pain. I wasn't going to take the risk that he was hurt and was either too scared or too ashamed to tell either me or my master that he needed to see a doctor."

Denton stared across at him. Benedict met his eyes without hesitation, obviously sure that he had done the right thing and not about to apologise for it.

Denton sighed. "Jerry would have done exactly the same thing in your place," he acknowledged.

"And what are you going to do now?" Peter asked.

The answer was obvious. "I'm going to fix this." That's what masters did. Denton didn't know exactly how he was going to do it, but he did know he was going to fix it—whatever it took.

Chapter Four

"I don't play games. If you're going to belong to me there will be no half measures."

Jerry forced himself to stay very still, sure the dominant wouldn't be impressed with a submissive who couldn't even kneel at his feet for two minutes without fidgeting. "I understand, sir."

Mr. Denton Greenwood stared down at him for several long seconds. Reaching forward he tucked a knuckle under his chin and tilted his head from side to side, examining him.

Jerry lifted his gaze and met the other man's eyes.

"Fullerton has explained the situation to you."

"Yes, sir." He'd been aware that Mr. Greenwood and his current master had been discussing the possibility of him moving under Mr. Greenwood's protection when they parted ways. He'd been aware of every damn second of that time, while he waited as patiently as he could to be brought in on the discussions.

"And what have you found out about me?" Mr. Greenwood asked.

Jerry blinked at him. "I trust my master's judgement, sir."

"And I trust you've had the sense to speak to the other subs,"
Mr. Greenwood said, a touch of amusement in his eyes.

Jerry dropped his gaze. The men he'd spoken to had been right.
Mr. Greenwood obviously knew the way things really worked.
"You're a good master. You respect safe words and limits. Your
punishments are harsh, but fair. Your previous submissives
speak very highly of you, sir," he recounted.

Mr. Greenwood nodded his acceptance of all that. "And you're
in favour of the arrangement?"

Jerry nodded. He hadn't found any reason not to be in favour
of it. "Yes, sir."

Mr. Greenwood looked past him, to where his current master
stood behind him. He nodded his approval to the other dominant.
In mere seconds, Fullerton had taken his collar off.

His new master took a new collar out of his pocket and put it
around his neck. Leaning back in his chair, the older man
studied the collar for a long time. "It will do until we decide if
the arrangement will be permanent," he announced.

Jerry swallowed, testing the feel of the leather around his neck.
It felt good. He hadn't enjoyed those seconds where his neck was
bare at all. "Thank you, sir."

"Master."

"Yes," Jerry agreed. "Thank you, master."

His new master stood up and led him out of the club. He was
aware of the dominant's eyes on him, watching to see if his new
pet had the sense not to look over his shoulder at his previous
master now that he belonged to another man. Jerry kept his eyes
forward, never looking to anyone other than his new master.

Thirty minutes later, they were in his new master's
apartment, standing in a very well equipped playroom. Shackles
hung from the centre of the room. Toys were arranged in neat
rows of hooks along one wall. A spanking bench stood in one
corner. Jerry didn't have time to take in a great deal else before
the first order came.

"Strip."

Jerry took his coat off. He was sure he'd hid his hesitation, but he couldn't stop a touch of colour rising to his cheeks. He knew it would get easier to strip down in front of the other man once he was more used to him, but no matter how many times he moved from the protection of a new master or mistress, the first time with a new dominant always left him blushing.

"Shy?" Mr. Greenwood asked.

Jerry felt his blush deepen.

"Look up."

He did as he was told.

The older man looked quietly amused. He brushed a knuckle over his cheek bone. "By the way you blush, no one would believe that you'd ever had a master."

Jerry was about to apologise, then he placed the tone of voice. Mr. Greenwood liked that idea. Suddenly mentioning that he was as experienced as any man who'd had over half a dozen previous masters and mistresses dropped to the bottom of his list of priorities.

His new master walked around him a few times while he stood in the middle of the room. Jerry took a deep breath and tried not to be nervous as he waited for a reaction. If the man made a fuss over him the way some masters were inclined to, he knew the blushing would just get worse.

Mr. Greenwood merely offered him a single nod of approval.

"Over the table."

He stepped forward without any hesitation and bent over the table that stood in front of the window. Automatically shifting his feet just over shoulder width apart so he was accessible to his master, he settled his hands behind his back.

"Neatly done," his master said, stepping up behind him.

He ran his hands across his shoulder and down his arms. When he reached his wrists, he moved them into a position that pleased him more. Jerry made a mental note of that as he began to push the details of the submission that had pleased his former *master out of his head and replace them with those that would please Denton.*

Slicked fingers slid against his exposed hole. No preamble, no hesitation. Complete confidence in the knowledge that neither was necessary. He was left in no doubt that he belonged to the other man. Jerry rested his cheek on the cold surface of the table as he felt a new sense of peace settle over him. He'd always had been quick to get a good sense of the men and women he submitted to. Denton felt different.

No, not just different – better. That sort of certainty of exactly who belonged to whom in the relationship was rarer than people thought. Jerry swallowed rapidly as his master's fingers rubbed against his prostate.

He bit his tongue but he couldn't hold back a whimper.

"Silence isn't required," Denton informed him.

"Thank you, sir."

The fingers slid away, three came back in their place, stretching him open wider. He wasn't in so much of a rush to settle them into their new roles that he wasn't taking the opportunity to get to know him. He wasn't rushing to top a body he wasn't familiar with.

Jerry wanted to feel his master inside him. He wanted that connection so badly he could taste it. But he lay exactly where his master wanted him and let the other man explore his body as he pleased.

Twenty minutes later his breaths were coming in pants, his eyes were closed so tight he could see stars behind his lids. Or maybe that had nothing to do with his eyes and everything to do with the fingers that were still playing inside him, along with the hand that had wormed its way under his stomach to wrap around his cock.

"Please, master," he whispered, unable to hold on to any sort of control.

Denton took his touch away. Jerry held his breath until he thought his lungs would explode with his need for oxygen, until he thought his mind would disintegrate with his sudden and overwhelming need for the other man. His desire to please and serve the other men and women he'd belonged to paled in comparison.

When his master's hand returned, they settled on his flanks and held him still. A blunt pressure pushed against his lubed up hole. Jerry took a deep breath, relaxing as his master pushed into him, slow and steady.

A few thrusts and Jerry knew there was no way he would be able to last long enough to impress the other man. There was only one thing he could do to at least show that he understood the sort of obedience that a master could rightly expect.

"Permission, master?" he stuttered out.

Another hard thrust set his prostate on fire. His teeth drew blood as they cut into his bottom lip as he scrambled for control. Another thrust and he knew it was a lost cause. Then, just in time –

"Come."

No master had ever given him any order that was easier to follow. Jerry came, hard and fast against the top of the padded table. His master must have been close to the edge too. As Jerry clenched around him, the older man buried himself deep inside him and yelled his own pleasure as he jerked and tightened his grip on his sides.

His master didn't rush to pull away from him, he stayed inside him as they caught their breath. When he eventually pulled away, he left him bent over the table while Jerry listened to the sounds of him tidying up his clothes.

"Up."

Jerry straightened up on command. His master steadied him as he turned him around to face him.

"I think this might work out very well, Jerry," Denton said after a while.

Jerry smiled up at the other man, "I'd like that, master. I – "

"It's Jerry, isn't it?"

Jerry blinked and did his best to focus back in on the real world. Tugging at his shirt collar he automatically tried to pull it further up his neck so it would cover the skin left bare since Denton took away his collar.

A quick glance at the posture and dress of the man standing next to him confirmed his status as a dominant. Jerry nodded. "Yes, sir."

"You used to belong to Denton Greenwood."

*Used to...*Jerry swallowed. A collar failed to shift around his wind pipe. He looked down. "Yes, sir."

The dominant frowned at the place where he'd scratched his skin in his haste to try to take his collar off. He reached out to touch the marks, as if trying to work out if they were serious and how they might have been inflicted. Jerry stepped back, a shot of alarm going through him at the unexpected contact with a stranger.

The man raised an eyebrow at him when he glanced up.

"I'm sorry, sir. I don't mean any offence, I..." He trailed off, having no idea how to explain that he wasn't pulling away from him in particular.

"If you're not ready to look for a new master, perhaps you shouldn't be in this sort of club tonight," he said. His tone was kind, as if he was worried about him rather than annoyed with him.

Jerry could only nod his agreement. If Mr. Vickery and Benedict hadn't insisted that he join them at the club, he would never have set foot in the place. Going to a leather bar without a collar around his neck was...he closed his eyes for a moment and suppressed a rush of emotion.

The older man looked down at him somewhat regretfully. Jerry hesitated, not sure what to say to him.

"Whose protection are you under now?" he asked.

"I'm staying with Mr. Vickery and Benedict until I..."

The man took out a business card and wrote something on the back of it. "For when you are ready to begin your search for a new master."

"Thank you, Mr. Nolan," he said, looking down at the small rectangle. Along with the name, the card indicated man was a barrister, evidently a very successful one if the address on the card was anything to judge by.

Mr. Nolan offered him a small smile and walked through into the lounge at the back of the club. Jerry stared blankly at the business card. He'd have to start looking for a master again at some point. A few years ago, he knew he wouldn't have hesitated to take Mr. Nolan up on his offer. When Mr. Fullerton had introduced him to Denton, it had never occurred to him that he should need to wait and try to clear his head before he could change his allegiance from one dominant to another.

If he hadn't been under the dominance of a man he loved for so long then...Jerry sighed and slipped the card into the back pocket of the jeans he'd borrowed from Benedict.

"You okay?" Benedict asked.

Jerry nodded and forced a smile as he turned towards the other man. "Are you having a good time?"

"Sure, I'm having a great time. Everyone seems to have crawled out of the woodwork. Caught up with a few guys I haven't seen for months." Benedict studied him carefully as he said it all, his mouth apparently working on automatic while his mind was on something else. "I noticed you were talking to Mr. Nolan for quite a while."

Jerry pushed his hands into his pockets to resist the temptation to reach up and rub his neck, to brush away any touch that didn't belong to his real master. He shrugged away his conversation with Mr. Nolan.

Benedict looked from him across to where Mr. Vickery stood by the bar. "There's someone else who wants to speak to you."

Jerry cleared his throat. "I'm not really...I mean, I haven't started looking for...I don't think I'm ready to..." he pushed his hands further into his pockets and wondered if there was somewhere quiet he could slip away to, so he could lose himself back in his daydreams.

Benedict continued to study him, no doubt waiting for him to actually finish a sentence at some point.

"I swear I'm not taking up permanent residence in your spare room. I'm looking for work, and I've got an interview next week, and I'll get my own place as soon as my first cheque comes in. I'm just not ready to start looking for a new master yet," he blurted out.

Benedict shook his head. "No! That wasn't what I meant. You know you're welcome to stay with us for as long as you want. We love having you with us. Trust me, having someone in the house who actually knows how to cook is fantastic!"

Jerry smiled slightly. Everything else might have fallen apart but the working for his keep part of the plan had proved wonderfully easy once he'd tasted Benedict's attempt at a home cooked meal.

"But I think you should at least hear this guy out," Benedict added. "No pressure or anything, I promise. Just listen to what he has to say?"

Holding back a sigh, trying to look at least vaguely interested in doing what the other submissive asked of him, Jerry nodded and let Benedict lead him towards the back of the club.

"He's in room seven."

Walking along side Benedict, Jerry hesitated when he realised that he was heading towards a private room and not into the lounge as he supposed. "I…" he trailed off as he realised what he was about to say made absolutely no sense. It was pointless to say his master would have a fit if he went into one of the clubs private rooms with another man. He didn't have a master.

Hurrying away from that thought, brought him quickly to a door with number seven marked on the front. He tapped on the door. It swung inwards a few inches. He looked across at Benedict, who nodded encouragingly. Seeing nothing else to do, Jerry pushed the door open a little further. A curtain hung over the doorway on the inside. Jerry tentatively moved the material back far enough to slip through the gap he created and step into the private space. The door swung nearly closed with the weight of the curtain.

"Hello?"

The room was almost pitch dark when the curtain dropped back into place behind him, sealing out the light from the ajar door. Only the shadowy outlines of a few pieces of furniture were visible in the muted light that made it in from somewhere. A few years ago he would have loved that sort of drama. Right then, he could have cheerfully done without it. His nerves were already shot. He didn't need anything making them worse.

Jerry cleared his throat and tried and hide his anxiety as he wondered if he was allowed to look for a light switch. "You wanted to speak to me, sir?" he asked the darkness, trying to make out the shape of a dominant somewhere in the room, but not even able to find the lines of the walls.

A bulb burst into life overhead. Blinking at the sudden explosion of light, Jerry's eyes went straight to the person kneeling in the floor in the middle of the room.

She was very beautiful, very naked and very…there. Jerry stared at her for several long moments trying to work out what the hell was going on and what Benedict could have been thinking.

The door clicked properly closed behind him. Jerry spun around. His throat closed up as he saw his master leaning against the curtains. Black material covered all the walls of the room hiding the door from anyone who couldn't remember where it was.

Jerry stared blankly at his former master. "I don't..." he whispered. "Benedict said..."

Denton looked him up and down, but made no move to approach him. "He and Peter have been taking good care of you?" he asked.

"They were driving past when I—" His gaze flashed up to meet his master's eyes. "You asked Mr. Vickery to take me in," he realised for the first time.

"Did you really think I'd leave you standing on the kerb?"

Jerry dropped his gaze to Denton's shoes. He stared at the polished leather for a long time before he could bring himself to speak. "I don't belong to you anymore, Mr. Greenwood. I don't expect you to ask your friends for favours on my account."

"You really think it ended as simply as taking off a collar?" Denton said. "Some things run even deeper than leather, Jerry. You should know that by now."

Jerry closed his eyes as he turned away from his master. When he opened his eyes again, they fell on the naked woman still kneeling with her head bowed in the middle of the room.

He looked back over his shoulder to his master for an explanation.

"She's for you," Denton said.

Jerry looked from him to the woman and back again.

"I can't belong to my master any more. I'm bi, and my belonging to him and being bi is just not possible anymore," Denton quoted at him, in a blank, emotionless tone of voice Jerry had never heard from him before.

Jerry looked to where he remembered the door being, wondering if Benedict was still on the other side of it, and if he could strangle him for repeating to his master what he'd told another submissive in confidence.

Turning his attention back to the woman, he tried to think of what he could say to her to explain this whole mess. Failing to find any words at all, he looked back to his master.

Denton never had learnt how to do things by halves. If he intended to accept that he was bi, he obviously wasn't going to play about with it. "I didn't ask you to find me a girl, master," he whispered.

"I may be far more besotted with you than a dominant should be, but I'm still your master, Jerry. If you occasionally have to have a woman in your life, perhaps I can learn to tolerate that. But she won't be a mistress. I won't hand you over to another dominant, male or female."

Each word was perfectly pronounced as Denton made an obvious and conscious effort to control his temper. It was also a lie. Jerry knew that, even if his master seemed able to fool himself. He wasn't tolerating anything. He hated the idea of anyone else laying a hand on his submissive just as much as Jerry did.

"I asked around. I spoke to men who've seen you with women. She's your type where women are concerned," he said.

Jerry shook his head looking from the naked woman — who was indeed his type — to his master and back again. "I didn't mean…I never asked you to find any sort of woman for me, master. I never said I wanted anyone but you."

Denton caught the woman's eye and nodded his dismissal, obviously not exactly heartbroken that Jerry wasn't going to take him up on the offer of her services for the rest of the night.

"Master! You can't just…" Jerry chided without thinking. He hurried across to the woman but he wasn't sure how to help her up without ending up putting his hands where he shouldn't. "Please get up. This is all just a huge misunderstanding. I'm really sorry. Where are your clothes?"

The woman looked past him to Denton then back to him. As she lifted her eyes and met his gaze, Jerry saw unexpected amusement shining in her expression. He studied her carefully, wondering if she was trying to hide some other emotion, but she didn't seem to be the least bit surprised or offended by the abrupt dismissal.

He looked back to his master, trying to work out if he was playing some sort of game with him. Denton looked equally surprised with her reaction once he focused in and noticed she was expressing anything at all.

"Peter told me you wouldn't be interested. Pity…" she said, looking Jerry up and down. Taking his hand to get to her feet she absentmindedly dusted off her knees as she continued. "You're sweet. He's hot. We could have all had some fun together."

Stepping over to a bit of curtain covered wall that didn't look at all different to the rest, she nudged the material aside and opened a door leading into a small storage space. Taking out a long coat and a pair of high heels, she put them all on.

Looking them both over one more time, she turned around and walked out of the room, finding the door through the curtains without the slightest hesitation.

Jerry took a step towards the door. "I should make sure she has cab fare or — "

Denton closed the door behind her and let the curtain fall back into place. "She's fine. Peter will no doubt see she gets to wherever she wants to go."

Jerry took another step towards the door anyway. "Then I should go back to Benedict and Mr...."

Denton stayed in front of the piece of curtain covering the door. He didn't appear to have any intention of moving out of his way.

Jerry shifted his weight back and forth from one foot to the other. He pushed his hands into his back pockets. A small rectangle of card stabbed into his palm. He snatched his hands away from it as if his master would somehow see that he'd taken a card from another man. Blushing bright red, he crossed his arms in front of him.

Denton was still studying him very carefully, the way a man might observe a frightened animal that might spook and run at the slightest sudden movement.

Jerry bit his lip, wondering what he should say. "How are you, sir?" he blurted out, as the silence demanded he fill it with something — with anything. He looked down, not sure if that sort of question was allowed now. It had been intended as a polite little query. It sounded more like a plea to be told every detail of everything his master had done since he'd taken his collar away.

Denton ignored the question. "Tell me why you left."

Jerry looked to the door behind the curtain. Denton didn't take his eyes off him.

"I had to go," he said.

"No!"

Jerry was shocked into meeting his master's eyes.

"No," Denton repeated more calmly. "I've heard that much before. I need to know *why*."

Jerry swallowed. "I couldn't stay," he said. Too late, he realised he'd only re-worded the answer that had annoyed his master so much before. "My staying with you was hurting you and—"

Denton stepped forward, he reached out to him, but he stopped just short of actually touching him. Jerry stood stock still, unable to bring himself to close that final little gap between them.

"You've never hurt me," Denton said, certainty about that fact clinging to ever syllable.

Jerry looked down. Denton was always very certain about everything. He'd miss that certainty so much. He cleared his throat. "Owning me was turning you into someone who... With me being who I am... I just couldn't... I had to..."

"Damn it, Jerry!"

He looked up at his master, eyes opened wide with shock. Denton closed his own eyes for a moment and Jerry could see how hard he was fighting to keep his temper.

"Whole sentences," the older man said, with obviously forced calm. "I know you find it hard sometimes. But if I'm going to understand whatever it is that you're trying to tell me, I need you to focus, and I need you to give me whole sentences. Okay?"

What he said was true, they had talked about it. Right at the start, before he'd even been given his permanent collar, let alone before he'd lost it. His master liked him to speak in whole sentences, even when it was difficult. Blushing when nervous was acceptable. Confusing his master was not.

Jerry turned away from the other man and paced around the room, trying to form his thoughts into something that would make sense outside his own head.

"Have you ever met someone who was homophobic, not just a prat who thinks those sorts of jokes are funny, the real thing?" he asked, as his pacing brought him to a stop in the middle of the room, his back to his master.

Denton frowned. "Of course."

"Someone who said things like homosexuality doesn't exist, or that it's a phase or it's a choice? Someone who told you it's wrong for you to be the way you are, that they thought less of you for not being straight?"

Denton's frown deepened.

Jerry turned back to his master, but he couldn't look him in the eye when he said it. He closed his eyes. "That day in the play room, you were one step away from picking up a placard calling me a sin against nature. And I know you're not that sort of man, master. But a bi man belonging to you was turning you into that sort of person and—"

"Jerry," Denton began.

Turning his back to his master in an effort to force himself to finish what he started saying, Jerry realised that Denton did deserve a real explanation and that he couldn't stop until it was given.

"You'd never have said those things before I belonged to you," Jerry whispered. "I couldn't stay to watch you turn into that sort of person. It would have been hell enough to watch the man I love turn into some petty minded bigot, but knowing I was at the root of it all. I just couldn't do that. I had to go. I had to."

Denton stopped within inches of touching Jerry. He stared down at the back of his bowed head and tried to think of something to say to take the hurt out of his lover's voice. He tried to think of the right words that would show Jerry the truth behind the things he'd said to him that night. It took far too long to bring the side of his personality that could talk about the situation rationally to the surface, but he finally managed it.

"I don't care who any man or woman wants to screw. As long as they're legal and consenting, I don't give a damn," he said, carefully.

Jerry continued to keep his back to him.

"Turn around, look at me."

He did as he was told, probably more from the habit of obeying his master than anything else, but Denton was willing to take would he could get.

"Look up."

He did that too. He looked so confused, so scared of everything. Denton's fingers twitched as he fought the instinct to pull him close and wrap his arms around him. He no longer had the right to do that. Jerry had made that quite clear when he stated that anything that happened between them would take place without his consent. The primitive, possessive part of Denton still wanted to do it so badly he could taste it.

"I can't let you turn into someone like that," Jerry whispered again, his eyes pleading with him for understanding. "I love you too much to let that happen, master."

Denton stared down at him. In all the reasons he'd dreamed up explaining Jerry's sudden departure, it had never occurred to him that he could believe he left for his master's benefit.

It never occurred to him that he might say he was bi because it was true either. But, as he listened to the emotions hanging on every word Jerry said, it became impossible to believe that he was clinging to a lie that made him feel better about being gay. It hadn't made him feel better. It hadn't made it easy. But, he still hadn't lied.

Denton closed his eyes for a moment as he realised his pet hadn't actually told him anything new. Everything he'd needed in order to see what Jerry said was the truth must have been there in his submissive from the start, but he'd never been willing to listen before. It had taken Jerry's panicked flight to scare the primal dominant inside him to admit the possibility Jerry could actually be telling the truth when he claimed the bi label.

Denton took a deep breath. If Jerry could calm himself enough to explain himself, it was about time he learnt to do the same.

"I'm your master."

Jerry went to speak. Denton silenced him with one raised hand. "You've had your say. Now it's your master's turn."

Jerry nodded his understanding. His lip would start bleeding if he didn't stop biting it soon.

"Sit down, and just listen." Denton directed him to the edge of the bed with a look. Jerry did as he was told, sitting down without trying to speak again.

Denton crouched in front of him, blocking any sort of escape route without actually touching him.

"Everything I said to you was about you and me, no one else. I don't give a damn about anyone else. Do I like the idea of *you* being bi? No." Denton sighed and looked down at his hands.

Jerry stayed silent and motionless. Denton was half sure he was even holding his breath.

"But none of it has bugger all to do with bi-phobia, pet. I'd be just as irrational if you announced a secret fetish for Australians or blonds or submissives or... or astronauts.

The rest of the world can screw who they want. But I don't want *you* to want anything your master isn't."

Jerry dropped his gaze.

"You belong to me, Jerry. And I'm hellishly possessive — you must know that by now. So, no, the idea that you could suddenly take it into your head that you want to run off with a woman — it doesn't sit well with me. Are you really that surprised?"

Jerry didn't raise his eyes.

Denton mentally rolled his eyes at himself. This was why dominants shouldn't fall in love with their submissives. Not only did it let them convince themselves they were in control enough of their own emotions to lead a scene when in hindsight they blatantly bloody well weren't, it also led to far too much soppiness, and to far too many situations that called for embarrassing confessions too.

Knowing all that, Denton pushed on regardless, thankful that he'd found a way to have this conversation with Jerry out of the earshot of the other men in the club if nothing else.

"Even if I wasn't in love with you, you're my ideal, pet — everything about you. Knowing that you can't say the same about your master is —"

"It doesn't work like that," Jerry cut in. "I know I'm supposed to wait my turn, master, but, please, it doesn't work like that."

Denton nodded once, giving him permission to continue.

"I'd love you just as much if you were a woman," Jerry blurted out. The words rushed together in his haste to have them heard, but they were whole words, whole ideas, which was always a welcome surprise when his pet was stressed. "The part of you I love isn't male or female.

I'm not in love with the part of you that makes you a man."

Denton couldn't help but raise an eyebrow at that.

Jerry seemed to realise what he'd said, and in spite of everything, he blushed. "I'm not saying I don't like your cock. You know that. I've begged for it often enough that you must know I..." He cleared his throat. "What I mean is, I belong to the bit of you that's you. I love the bit of you that is *you*. It's not about wanting men and women, I'm attracted to people — they happen to be men or women, but I really don't care one way or the other."

Denton stayed still and silent, wary that any move might spook his lover and stop the steady flow of words. If he could just keep Jerry able to offer up full sentences, and himself able to keep a lid on his anger, they might have a chance.

"I don't think of you as a man, master. I don't think of you as a dominant or British or someone who's tall or dark or anything else. You're you. You're my master and I love you. Nothing else matters. I can't change any of that. I can't lie about it."

Denton met his eyes and he saw the truth in them, not just in those words he'd said out loud, but in the words he kept back as well. He heard the desperate need to be understood, to have that part of his psyche recognised and accepted.

Jerry swallowed rapidly, as if his emotions were about to get the better of him. Denton nodded his understanding, releasing him from the pressure to try to explain anything any further.

He knew what he needed to know now. He knew what had to happen next. For once, every part of his mind agreed easily on one course of action. He stood up and Jerry rose to his feet too.

It took more strength of will than Denton was aware he possessed to take a step back from him.

"Master?" Jerry asked. He reached out. He offered himself to him, but he stopped short of actually touching him, giving his master the right to reach out and make the final contact as and when he chose.

Denton stared down at him for a long time before he could make his throat work and be sure his words would come out slow and steady and dominant. "You should go and find Peter and Benedict. It's getting late. No doubt they'll want to go home soon."

"I..."

For several long seconds, Jerry looked up at him, hope burning then dying in his eyes. His gaze dropped to his hand as it fell back to his side. A moment later his hand rose to his throat, sliding against his bare neck, following the line where his old collar had caressed his skin. He laid his hand over the side of his neck as if trying to protect the suddenly vulnerable skin from further damage.

He looked up at Denton again, so hurt and obviously so embarrassed to have said all that only to be turned away. If Denton had any doubt over how many people Jerry had given that explanation to, they evaporated. He knew he was the only one Jerry had said those words too. In spite of all that, Denton forced himself to stay perfectly still.

Jerry pawed at the curtains until he found the door and left the room in silence, closing the door quietly behind him on the way out. Denton leaned against the wall next to the door and stared at the empty room without really seeing it.

It was better for Jerry that his master should send him away. He knew that. It still didn't stop him feeling like a complete bastard.

Chapter Five

"I really don't mind staying here by myself," Jerry tried
again.

"It will do you good to get out of the house." Benedict
took a shirt out of his wardrobe and held it in front of
Jerry, checking the tone against his skin.

Jerry didn't need to check. He knew it was the perfect
colour for him. His master had bought him an almost
identical shirt, and he'd never failed to quietly nod his
approval every time he saw him wearing it.

"You and Mr. Vickery should go by yourselves," Jerry
suggested. "I know it must be hard for both of you, having
a stranger in your house all the time, and..."

Benedict brushed that aside. "We both love having you
here." He considered the colour of the shirt again and laid
it out on the bed before he extracted a pair of jeans and a
pair of boots from the wardrobe to go with them.

They were all almost indistinguishable from the clothes
his master had bought him to wear while he lived with

him. Jerry was sure Benedict meant it for the best, trying to give him things that were familiar, but it didn't help. It just made it all the harder to push away the memories that constantly threatened to over-power him. There were days when he got dressed and he was sure he could smell his master's aftershave on clothes that had never been anywhere near his master.

"We'll have to do something with your hair," Benedict said.

"My master never liked me to—" Jerry cut himself short. His master had made it quite clear that he liked to be able to run his hands through his hair without getting stabbed by gel spikes or tangled in some complicated style. Jerry shook his head at himself as he tried and failed to convince himself that Denton's opinion wasn't important any more. "Whatever you think is best."

Benedict hesitated. "It looks great as it is."

Jerry closed his eyes. Benedict was being nice. Mr. Vickery and Benedict were both being very nice and very kind to him, which just made him feel even worse for not being at all inclined to go out to a club with them that night. "Benedict?"

The other submissive made a noncommittal sound as he fussed about setting the things on Jerry's bedside table straight.

"You and your master haven't...you're not trying to set me up with anyone, are you?"

"Why would you think that?"

"Benedict..." Jerry began. Just because he knew that Denton had no intention of taking him back, that didn't mean he could just flip a switch and be ready to look for a new master or mistress.

Benedict fixed a bright smile onto his lips. "Why don't you just get ready? You'll feel much more cheerful when you get to the club and see everyone."

Jerry pinned an equally fake smile to his own lips and nodded.

* * * *

"You like that, don't you, pet?"

Jerry nodded as the blush raced to his cheeks. He'd long ago given up on the idea he would ever be able to submit to his master without seeing the older man's lips quirk in amusement at his heightened colour. At least at that moment, his head was bowed and, although Denton would inevitably guess it was there, he couldn't actually see it.

His master's hand came down on his other buttock. Jerry closed his eyes. An image flashed up before his eyes of stark red hand marks on pale skin. His collar shifted around his throat as he rocked forward. He let out a whimper.

Denton stroked his palm over the heated skin on his backside. His hand disappeared for a second before it connected first to his right cheek then to his left in quick succession.

Sharp spikes of pleasure raced through Jerry's body. He arched his back, pushing his backside out for more as his master went back to stroking him very gently. His movements made no difference to his lover's touch. He received exactly what his master wanted him to – no more, no less.

"I remember someone telling me that he didn't like to be spanked," Denton mused.

Giving up on getting a firmer touch until his master was quite ready to provide one, Jerry squirmed forward again. The restraints built into the spanking bench didn't allow him much freedom. He couldn't obtain even the slightest friction against his aching cock. All he could do was wait upon his master's pleasure.

Two more quick spanks and Denton's knuckle stroked down between his buttocks and across his hole. Jerry bit his lip to hold back a plea. It felt like months rather than days since his master had let him come.

His legs were held apart, each knee resting on its own padded support as his upper body lay across another leather covered surface. It might have been labelled 'spanking' but it always seemed to Jerry that the man who designed it had never intended the submissive strapped to the beautiful structure to be available just for that.

He knew it would be hours before Denton would likely make use of the inviting position the bench placed him in. He liked to build up the heat slowly. His master liked to watch him squirm and hear him beg before he gave him what the spanking made him crave more than anything – a hard cock pressed against his hole rather than a bare knuckle.

Just as he expected, his master's attention didn't linger there very long. His hand dropped further down between his legs. His fingers stroked his balls.

"You haven't answered my question."

Jerry frowned, trying and failing to pull the scattered pieces of his mind together and focus on anything that wasn't the warm hand palming his testicles.

"Master?" he managed to stutter out.

"You told me you didn't like being spanked."

Jerry whimpered again. He swallowed rapidly as he scrambled for control. "That was before, master."

"Before what?" Denton asked, still manipulating the tight sacs.

"Before you," Jerry whispered.

Denton was silent for a few seconds, but Jerry could feel his mood change and he knew his master was pleased with the answer. He liked being spanked by his master. Denton was the only man or woman he had ever belonged to that could make it feel like it wasn't a punishment. With Denton it felt perfect.

No other words were spoken on the subject. Denton released his handhold on his sacs and went back to stroking his buttocks. A few seconds later his hand struck. This time it was different. No more teasing. His honest answer had obviously earned him the pleasure of a proper spanking. Denton set up his rhythm, alternating between cheeks, coating the skin with an even layer of heat that soaked into his body and sent pleasure shooting through his veins.

Ten minutes later, he was half sure that his master was determined to make him come from nothing more than his hand striking his arse. But, he was only half sure. If he was wrong, Denton might be angry with him for spoiling his plans for something else.

Jerry whimpered at the idea. With his master's approval still strong in his mind, the last thing he wanted was for Denton to suddenly be disappointed in him.

"Permission?" he whispered. "Please?"

"Permiss — "

"Hello again."

It took Jerry several long seconds to focus back in on reality, but his smile for Mr. Nolan was slightly more genuine than it had been for any of the dozens of other men who approached him that night and pulled him from his memories. "Hello, sir."

The older man smiled down at him rather sympathetically. "Come and sit with me." It was definitely an order not an invitation.

Jerry hesitated for a moment before he followed the other man. When Mr. Nolan sat on one of the stools that lined the bar, Jerry didn't immediately hop up onto the stool next to him, and not just because he hadn't received an order to do so.

"Sir, I don't mean to be impolite," he began.

"I'm not suggesting you should offer me your submission."

Jerry hesitated again.

"You're obviously not ready for anything like that. But I've been watching you for over an hour, and as the evening wears on, it's increasingly painful to see you trying to nod and smile politely at all the dominants hitting on you. No one will bother you while you are speaking to me."

Jerry looked at the stool.

"You don't need my permission."

"Thank you, sir." Jerry slipped up onto the bar stool, placing his Coke on the dark wooden surface. He stared into his drink not sure what an uncollared submissive was supposed say to a dominant who he wasn't hoping would be his master.

"When was the last time you were without a master?" Mr. Nolan asked him.

"The day before I turned legal," Jerry whispered. "I've never really been without a dominant." He held onto his glass very tightly, trying not to give in to the temptation to cover his bare neck, trying not to retreat into the memories he'd hid in more and more often over the last few days.

"It must be hard."

Jerry swirled his drink a little. "I never realised how hard it would be," he whispered. "How lost I would feel. Maybe it's...I cared for my other dominants, but I wasn't in love with them, sir. Not like with my...with Mr. Greenwood."

"That's why you're taking some time before you look for a new master this time around?"

Jerry nodded. "Maybe I should look for a mistress instead," he mused.

"You're bi then?"

He nodded again. "I wish I wasn't, but..." He sighed and wished he had a stronger drink in front of him, too. His master had let him have a drink or two now and then, not enough to get properly drunk, but just the right amount to get a bit happy on it. "Mr. Vickery said that I wasn't to drink anything with any alcohol in it."

He glanced across and saw that Mr. Nolan was watching him with obvious appreciation and no small touch of amusement.

"I'm sorry, sir, I really don't know how to talk to anyone when I'm like this."

"You're doing fine."

Jerry turned his attention back to his drink.

"Tell me about Greenwood."

"Why?" Jerry asked, suddenly unsure he should be talking to the dominant at all.

"Because you're obviously still in love with him."

"He doesn't want me anymore, sir," Jerry said.

"Does he know how you feel about him?"

Jerry nodded. "I told him," he whispered. He must have said it a dozen times in that back room as he struggled to make his master understand.

"And what did he say?"

Jerry shook his head, unwilling to let memories of that night in the club back into his head. Happier memories were allowed to linger as long as they wanted, but nothing to do with that night when he'd finally had to admit to himself that it was over forever. He couldn't think of that and stay sane.

"Why are you being so nice to me, sir?"

"Because you seem to need to talk to someone who isn't trying to screw you. And because you remind me of someone," Mr. Nolan said.

Jerry turned to him, latching on to the hope that talking about someone else's memories might push that night out of his head. "Who, sir?"

"His name was Frank."

"Was?" Jerry asked.

"He died last year."

"Oh...I'm sorry, sir."

Mr. Nolan nodded once in acceptance of his sympathy, but he seemed to have reached the stage where he was resigned to the facts of the matter.

"He belonged to you?" Jerry asked, cautiously.

"Yes, for the best part of a lifetime."

"Was it...?" Jerry trailed off. A tendency to blurt things out when he was nervous really didn't excuse some questions.

"AIDs?" Mr. Nolan asked. "No, nothing like that. A car accident. He was sober. The other driver wasn't."

"I'm sorry, sir," Jerry said again.

"He was very like you."

Jerry nibbled at his lip. "Would it make you feel better if I—?" He cut himself off, not even knowing what he had intended to offer the other man. Before he'd belonged to Denton he wouldn't have thought twice about offering such a dominant whatever he wanted. Now, it was different.

Mr. Nolan smiled half sadly, but still with a touch of amusement in his eyes. "I think that this is one of those times when it's best for misery not to take advantage of its company."

Jerry nodded and turned back to his drink. In a weird sort of way sitting with Mr. Nolan was comforting. The older man didn't expect him to be happy. He didn't expect him to be able to cope or to be able to bounce back into the game and find another master as easily as he would pick out a new book from the library.

For the first time since he'd left his master's protection, Jerry felt a tiny bit of peace settle around him. For a few moments, the whole mess seemed survivable. If Mr. Nolan had survived losing Frank, then maybe there was hope for him yet.

"Gentlemen, your attention, please!"

Jerry turned towards the small stage at the other end of the room, where public announcements and punishments were conducted. Every other man in the room did the same. The ripple of chatting voices hushed to a murmur. The bartender got down from the stage to let the man who'd requested the opportunity to make a public announcement, get up onto the raised platform in his place.

All the blood drained from Jerry's face as he watched his master's head and shoulders appear over the top of the crowd. From the far side of the room, he automatically tried to make out the head of another man waiting to step onto the platform with him.

There was only one reason why his master would step up there that night—to give a new collar to a new submissive, to make Jerry's replacement official. All the air rushed out of the room. Jerry wanted to close his eyes, but his body wasn't obeying his orders. His eyes stayed wide open, staring across the room at his master.

He scrambled at his store of memories, trying to latch on to some happy moment and pull it tight around him like a protective little shell. It didn't work. Blocking out the rest of the world was one thing. He couldn't ignore his master.

"Jerry," he heard someone say to his left.

He couldn't remember who was sitting there. He couldn't tear his gaze away from his master to look. Standing up, he took a shaky step forward, not sure where he was trying to go. All he knew was that he couldn't sit there and watch his master fall in love with someone else right there on the stage in front of him.

A hand gripped his arm, stopping him short. Jerry followed the arm attached to the hand until he reached a pair of concerned blue eyes. He took a step away from Mr. Nolan, because the older man wasn't his master, and because that's what a submissive was supposed to do when a man who wasn't his master took hold of him.

He didn't bother to take a second step away, by that time he'd remembered there wasn't any point. "It's really over," he whispered.

Mr. Nolan looked sadly down at him, obviously not sure what to say. Jerry stared back up at him. It could be worse. If he had to find a new master, he could do a lot worse than accept a collar from Mr. Nolan. He would make a kind, and probably an indulgent, master. Jerry was sure the dominant would give him time to get over Denton before he expected anything more than quiet companionship from him. Filling the gap that his previous submissive's death had left in Mr. Nolan's life would be—

"I have an announcement to make." Denton's voice cut through every sound in the room and every thought in Jerry's head, calling Jerry to his side. He turned back towards his master, staring at him through blurry eyes as he looked across the room.

He swayed slightly and felt Mr. Nolan put his arm around his shoulders, supporting him in case he should buckle completely before this horrible charade was over.

"The way gossip spreads around this place, I'm sure you're all well aware that, as of two weeks ago, Jerry Clarke was released from my protection."

A murmur went through the crowd. Jerry lifted his hand to cover his neck as the men closest to him turned to stare. Mr. Nolan's arm tightened around him, silently offering him his support.

"It wasn't a break or a trial or any of that bull. It was a permanent separation."

Jerry's hand rubbed at the skin on his neck. It burned all around where his collar should have been.

"I've always believed that it's a master's place to possess, and it's a submissive's place to belong to his master in every way one man can belong to another. In *every* way," he stressed.

Jerry dropped his gaze and stared at the floor just in front of his feet.

"Love doesn't come into it. That's best left to the vanilla boys who don't understand what leather really means. Love doesn't come into it, until you're fool enough to actually fall in love with the man under your protection."

Jerry closed his eyes. Denton always did things at a far faster pace than the rest of the world. If he was able to bounce back into the game this soon, there was no reason why he shouldn't have already found time to fall in love with his new submissive, too.

"And then possessing is not enough, controlling a man is not enough. Suddenly it's vital that you fill the other man's entire world, and to make a complete bastard out of yourself in the process."

For a few moments, silence filled the room. Denton ran his eyes over the crowd, as if wanting to be sure that everyone was giving him their complete attention before he continued.

"I live in a world that's black and white. Dominant and submissive, top and bottom, gay and straight. I never expected to fall in love with a man who didn't see the world in the same way as me."

The first time his master had ever said that he loved him out loud in front of anyone else, and it was only to tell everyone he wasn't a good enough submissive to keep that love. Jerry lifted his eyes and looked at all the men staring at him. Everyone was going to think that Denton had disowned him because he'd forgotten his place as a submissive, that his submission wasn't good enough to keep.

Jerry turned his back on his former master, on the man standing up on that stage and neatly destroying his chances of ever finding another good man to belong to. He looked up at Mr. Nolan, hoping his master's words hadn't already put the older man off.

"If your offer is still open, sir, I'd be honoured if you'd let me belong to you."

Mr. Nolan smiled slightly and stroked his cheek with the back of his knuckles. When he saw the look in his eyes, Jerry knew he was making the right decision. Mr. Nolan would be a good master. Mr. Nolan wouldn't make him stay there and listen to any more of what his previous master said to the rest of the room.

Chapter Six

Denton scanned the crowd for what felt like the thousandth time but he still failed to catch sight of the reason why he was standing up on that little stage making a damn fool of himself.

All his well rehearsed words ran around in his head swirling together so fast, he was half sure that nothing he said made any sense at all. He wished like hell he hadn't been too proud to write out some cue cards. He wished he'd managed to catch a glimpse of Jerry so he could be sure that Peter and Benedict had succeeded in dragging him to the club that night.

Swallowing down any stutter before it could make itself into his words, Denton pushed on.

"But sometimes the best things in love aren't simple. They aren't black or white. And sometimes the best men aren't simple either. Sometimes they aren't even straight or gay."

Another sweep of his eyes across the room and he still couldn't see him. He'd assumed Jerry would have been well visible by this point. He'd imagined that his lover would have been right at the front of the crowd and he would have been able to look into Jerry's eyes while he made such a soppy, bloody fool of himself.

It never occurred to him that he would have had to make his confession to a room full of men and not even be able to judge how well his apology was going down with his lover.

Denton took a deep breath. Feeling more foolish than he ever had in his life, he forced himself to keep going.

"I've only ever had one idea of what my perfect submissive would be like. Jerry is my ideal in every way. My ideal lover. My ideal submissive. My ideal man. He's the only man I've ever really loved. That's why I'm up here asking him to forgive me. That's why I'm asking him to come back under my protection, even though I don't fulfil the same single simple ideal for him."

Taking a length of black leather from his back pocket, he held it up so the silver buckle could catch the light of all those shining bulbs pointing directly at the stage. The leather felt stiff and unfamiliar in his hand. For a moment he had the horrible feeling that those in the front row might notice his fingertips tremble as he held the collar out for everyone to see.

"Jerry, if you accept my protection, come back to your master," he said.

The room was deadly silent. Every one of the men in the club, dominant and submissive alike, seemed to stare at the collar and hold his breath as they all waited for Jerry to step forward and give Denton his answer.

The silence stretched on. Men began to look around, whispering to their neighbours. Denton stayed frozen where he was, waiting in front of the whole club for any sign of Jerry.

Another minute passed, and Denton started to wonder what the worst case scenario was. That he'd just said all that to a crowd of men that didn't actually include his submissive, or that Jerry was there, but wasn't able to forgive him.

The idea of Jerry being there but having no interest in joining him on the stage made a cold sweat break out on his skin. He could live with making a fool of himself for someone who wasn't there. Hell, Denton was pretty sure he could even get back up on the stage and do this bloody stupid stunt again on another night when Jerry *was* there.

But Jerry had to forgive him once he saw it. He had to, because Denton had no doubt that Jerry would have taken him back while they stood in the back room of the club a week ago.

Denton looked out over the men again. They were starting to get restless and nervous on his behalf now. Denton cursed himself for a fool.

He should have collared Jerry back there, when they were alone in that room together. Any sane man would have brought a man like Jerry back to his heel at the very first chance that came his way. But no, he had to get some stupid idea that Jerry needed to see his master pay his penance, that he needed to hear him say his apology as publicly as he'd dismissed bisexuality so many times in the past, and now...

At the back of the room, a man looked over his shoulder and stepped to one side. Another man did the same. Like dominos, the men down the centre of the room parted as someone smaller than them nudged his way through the crowed space. By the time the ripple had reached half way down the room, the men ahead of the wave were ahead of the game and stepping back to make way.

Jerry stepped between the men, the club lights illuminating every inch of his naked body. Eyes lowered, he walked barefoot across the floor, and knelt on the edge of the stage in front of his master.

The murmur of voices cut back to silence. Denton stared down at the top of Jerry's head. Still frozen in place, he didn't know how to reach out to him. Right then he wasn't sure he had the courage to risk his lover pulling away from him as he had that horrifying night back at their house.

Jerry silently bowed down in front of him until his head rested on the floor barely an inch in front of his master's feet, filling the gap in proceedings when his master fought to pull himself together as if it was all part of some perfectly choreographed scene worked out months in advance.

"As you were," Denton said. The words seemed to echo around the silent room.

Jerry rose once more to his knees, his hands hanging idly at his sides, his head still bowed.

"Look at your master."

Jerry slowly tilted his head back, letting his master see his face and look directly into his eyes. They were so full of emotion, Denton reached for him without thinking about anything more than a need to comfort the younger man.

"Good boy," he whispered.

The hand holding the collar up seemed to come back to life. Denton lowered the leather to his pet's neck.

"This is what you want?" the objective part of his brain forced him to ask.

"Yes, master," Jerry whispered back, his voice almost cracking with pure relief.

The possessive side couldn't wait any longer. The leather was fastened in place in seconds. All sign of nervous tremble gone from his fingers, Denton smoothed the blackness into place around his pet's neck, checking the fit.

Jerry swallowed and let out a deep breath as he closed his eyes. A small smile made its way to his lips just before his teeth caught the tender skin and nibbled at it in an effort to keep his emotions in check.

Denton stroked his hand through Jerry's hair tugging him forward a little so the younger man could rest his head against his hip. Jerry leaned eagerly into his touch in a way Denton had been convinced he'd lost forever.

Tearing his eyes away from the beautiful sight kneeling at his feet, Denton looked at the crowd of men, catching the eyes of the dominants, making sure that everyone was nice and sure Jerry belonged to him again. Slowly the crowd started to dissipate and turn back in on themselves as they realised the show was essentially over.

"Up you get," Denton ordered after a while.

Jerry rose gradually to his feet. Not willing to let him go, Denton kept his fingers tangled in Jerry's hair. A moment after he reached his full height, Jerry was firmly wrapped in the circle of his master's arms, with his face tucked into the crook of his neck. The small man held on to his shirt so tight, the fabric cut into Denton's skin.

Smiling, Denton pressed a kiss onto the top of Jerry's head. "Good pet, that's right. I've got you."

Jerry nodded but didn't lift his face to speak. He pressed a kiss onto Denton's neck instead.

The hand he'd buried in Jerry's hair dropped down to his neck, to stroke the leather encircling his skin.

Jerry pulled away the tiniest fraction, just enough that he could quickly look up into his master's eyes before dropping his gaze again. "It's new, master," he observed softly, lifting his hand to join Denton's on the stiff leather.

"Yes," Denton agreed.

Jerry nodded and stopped short of actually questioning his decision to replace the old collar.

"A new start," Denton clarified.

Jerry nodded again and burrowed back closer into his master's arms.

"Cold, pet?"

Jerry shook his head. "It just feels like everyone's staring at my arse, master," he murmured into his shoulder.

Denton chuckled. "You stripped naked and got on stage in the middle of a leather bar, Jerry. Of course everyone's staring at your arse." He ran one of his hands down the submissive's back and cupped the firm, round muscle in the palm of his hand. Something eased inside him as Jerry accepted his touch without protest or comment. Denton smiled as his possessive side gloried in the simple pleasure that came with the freedom to touch his lover however he wanted.

Someone cleared his throat. Denton looked over Jerry's shoulder and saw an older dominant set a small pile of clothes—of Jerry's clothes—on the corner of the stage.

Jerry turned to look over his shoulder too. "Mr. Nolan," he said. "Thank you, I…"

When he would have turned around, Denton's hands on his neck and his backside kept him in place.

"Mr. Nolan let me sit with him," Jerry said softly. "He was very kind to me."

Denton looked across to the other man. A flash of recognition hit him, and he remembered seeing a man who looked very much like Jerry with him on a great many occasions in the past. Jerry tugged slightly at his shirt. Looking down into his eyes, Denton saw the sympathy there.

He pushed the instinct to make it clear who Jerry belonged to away. "Thank you for looking after him until I could bring him back to me," Denton said instead.

Obvious relief flooded through Jerry. He rested his head on his master's shoulder as Denton exchanged a few more words with the other man. Mr. Nolan didn't linger for very long before he made his excuses and walked away.

"Car accident," Jerry whispered.

Denton pressed another kiss onto his temple. "Yes. Frank. I remember. He was a good man."

"Do you think Michael looks like me?"

Denton managed to call to mind a young blond man Jerry had been speaking to on the same night everything went to hell for them. "A little like you," he said. "But more like Frank. Playing match maker for Nolan, pet?"

Jerry looked up at him and, when he'd confirmed that his master was definitely teasing, smiled. "Do you think Michael would make a nice submissive for him, master?"

"Perhaps," Denton allowed. "I'll mention Nolan to Phillips next time I see him. If he thinks they'll suit each other, he'll see that they are introduced."

"Thank you, master."

"But first, you're going to tell me exactly what he was doing with all your clothes?" Denton told him, making sure Jerry would hear the teasing note linger in his voice. He was so lightheaded with relief at having Jerry back where he belonged, he couldn't help but tease.

Jerry bit his lip. "I didn't want to come to you wearing clothes another man gave me," he whispered. "I'm sorry I made you wait. You could punish me for that, and for everything I said to you that night, and..."

Denton put a fingertip to his lips. "There's no punishment. But I swear if you do this to me again, I'll turn you over my knee so quickly, there wouldn't be time for you to mutter anything about 'having to go' without giving me a damn good reason first."

Jerry nodded.

Denton stared down at him. "I'll respect your safe word, Jerry, but I won't let you leave again without actually telling me what the hell is wrong—never again, understand."

He nodded once more. "Maybe I should put my clothes on now, master?" he suggested.

"No."

Jerry glanced into his eyes and nodded his acceptance of his decision.

"And on that subject, there will be no more of this bull about it being my apartment, your name's on the bloody lease right next to mine. And I'll be damned if I'll spend half my time fetching and carrying all the clothes you're so damn convinced that I own back and fore to you, if you happen to spend a few days away from our house again."

Jerry looked at his clothes, still piled on the edge of the stage.

Denton chuckled. "They didn't seem more than a little familiar?"

Jerry blushed and stroked his fingers along his master's shirt. "Take me home, master?" he asked.

Denton wrapped his hand around Jerry's wrist, studying his face to see his reaction. The younger man closed his eyes as if he was savouring the moment.

"We're going home now," Denton informed him.

Jerry nodded. Denton only stopped for the briefest moment to let Jerry pick up his clothes before he led him briskly out of the club.

In the car park he put Jerry into the passenger side of his car and strode quickly around to the driver's seat. He had neither the patience nor the inclination for anything fancy. "Put your belt on. You have until the car stops to put on whatever clothes you want to wear on the way up to our apartment. I'm not waiting for you once I turn the engine off."

"Yes, master."

Jerry put his seatbelt on and quickly began to sort through his clothes. As far as he remembered he'd just dropped them on the floor where he'd stood, but Mr. Nolan had put them in a nice neat little pile for him when he collected them.

They weren't far from their apartment, and Denton was putting his foot down. At that time of night, there wasn't much traffic to get in their way. Jerry thought he could just about get everything on if he hurried, and the traffic lights went his way.

Holding his jeans in one hand and his shoes in the other, he hesitated. An idea started to form inside his head. He looked across at his master's profile. It wasn't in him to ask for anything from Denton right then. He was back with his master, wanting anything more than that would be greedy. But his master had never been slow on the uptake and he couldn't help but drop a hint about his idea. Jerry pulled his jeans on and put everything else, shoes and all, in a neat little pile on his lap.

Denton glanced across and raised an eyebrow at him.

Jerry stared straight ahead and took a deep breath, realising that he was inviting a hell of a lot of trouble to fall down all around him if this went wrong.

In the car park, Jerry waited as his master walked around to his side of the car and took hold of his wrist once more. His master didn't turn around and look at him until he closed the apartment door behind them.

"You really do believe in second chances, don't you, pet?" Denton asked.

Jerry stared at his master's shoulder, not able to tell his master's opinion of his conduct from his tone of voice.

"Playroom," he whispered in Jerry's ear. "Naked. Central shackles. Go."

Jerry hurried into the play room and got himself ready for his master. He was soon standing exactly where he had stood on another Saturday night a whole lifetime ago. Denton made him wait again. Standing under the shackles, Jerry could only hope like hell he hadn't made the biggest mistake of his life by suggesting a rehash of the one scene that had come so close to ruining him.

His master finally pushed the door open. He strode in as if he wasn't the least bit nervous about repeating the scene. His confidence soothed Jerry a little.

"I'm not playing games tonight. If I ask you a question I want a full and honest response. Lies and omissions will both be punished harshly," Denton announced.

"Yes, master," Jerry whispered.

"When was the last time you thought about having sex with someone who wasn't your master?" he demanded.

Jerry watched his master pace. He hadn't put the shackles on, but he didn't seem to be aware of that neglected part of the procedure. Jerry wasn't sure if there was a polite way to bring that to his master's attention.

"Thinking time is acceptable, day dreaming time is not."

"I thought about it a lot over the last few weeks, master," Jerry whispered. "But not the way you mean."

"Oh?"

"I wasn't thinking about it to enjoy it. I thought I'd probably need to — to find a new master," he looked down.

Honesty. He couldn't deny his master that. "I thought I might need to for money at one point, too."

Denton moved closer him, stopping barely a foot away from contact. "You thought I'd let that happen?"

Jerry couldn't lift his gaze. "Everything had fallen apart and I didn't have a master and I…I was scared. I always imagine the worst when I'm scared, master. I try not to, but I can't help it."

"Like imagining that I'd force you?" Denton asked.

An embarrassed blush raced to Jerry's cheeks. "I didn't really mean it to sound like that. I knew I wouldn't leave if I got too close to you. I had to push you away as hard as I could, or I would have stayed, and I thought staying would make you think like that and…"

Denton stroked his cheek, gentling him down as his words began to tumble out too quickly to be understood. "And now you know differently, don't you, pet?"

Jerry nodded.

"I can accept that you're bi, Jerry."

Jerry nodded again, holding the words close and savouring them.

"Although the part of you I'm in love with isn't bi."

As quickly as embarrassment had coloured his cheeks, Jerry felt the blood drain away. It couldn't happen again. It couldn't…

"Master?"

"Look at me," Denton ordered.

Jerry looked up at his master. Denton stroked his hair back from his eyes in a familiar gesture. Jerry accepted it, just as he always welcomed his master's touch. Denton smiled slightly as if he'd suddenly won something amazing.

"The part of you that I'm in love with is the part of you that's *you*. And that isn't gay or bi or straight or anything else."

Jerry closed his eyes at hearing his own thoughts quoted back at him. Blood began to move through his veins again. His lungs dragged another dose of air into his body.

"If I can accept that the part of me that you love isn't male or female, you'll just have to face the fact that the part of you that I love isn't gay or bi. Although, you'll also have to learn to live with the fact I'm still bloody glad that no part of you is entirely straight. I'm not hetrophobic either, pet, but I think I'm well within my rights in expecting my lover to have at least a passing interest in men."

Jerry nodded his agreement, relief making him smile.

As he spoke, his master had lowered his head. His lips were just a fraction of an inch away from offering him a kiss.

"Please, master?" Jerry whispered.

"First you have to do something for me," Denton whispered. "Three little words."

Jerry closed his eyes and took a leap of faith. "I love you, master."

Denton lips brushed against Jerry's as he smiled. "Technically that's four words, but I'll let you off this time."

He touched their mouths together, very gently. Jerry parted his lips and his master slowly accepted his invitation, gradually deepening the kiss until Jerry couldn't help but whimper and moan into his master's mouth.

Jerry couldn't remember the last time a kiss, even one from his master, made him honest to God weak at the knees. He dropped his hands from their place next to the shackles and wrapped his arms around his master's neck, holding on, both for support, and just for the joy of feeling his master holding him close in return. If he got turned over the other man's knee for moving without permission, he didn't care. It would be worth it.

When Denton broke the kiss he looked at Jerry's hands resting on his shoulders and raised an eyebrow.

"Sorry, master," Jerry gasped. "I forgot to ask you to put the shackles on me."

"If I'd wanted them on you, you wouldn't have had to remind me."

Jerry hesitated, not sure if he'd done something wrong or not.

"If bondage is the only thing that keeps you where I want you, your inability to stand on your own two feet while you kiss me is the least of our problems."

Wrapping his hand around Jerry's wrist in what Jerry was quickly coming to think of as the best hold anyone could ever take on him, Denton led him into their bedroom and nudged him towards the bed before he could think of anything to say in response.

"Make your choice, Jerry."

"Master?" Jerry frowned his confusion as he automatically got onto the bed and waited for another order.

"I made you an offer a few weeks ago. I'm a man of my word. Make your choice."

"I never said I was gay," Jerry blurted out as he watched his master drop his clothes on the floor by the side of the bed until he was just as naked as his submissive. His eyes flickered all over the older man's body. It felt like decades had passed since he'd seen him that way. The fact he was hard and obviously ready to remind Jerry exactly who he belonged to was just the icing on the cake.

Denton shrugged. "You told me that you'll never belong to a woman again. It's close enough as far as I'm concerned."

Getting up onto his knees, Jerry knelt right on the edge of the bed, but he was still not quite within touching distance of his master.

"Anything you want," Denton reminded him stepping closer so he stood right in front of Jerry.

"Honest," Jerry repeated back his master's earlier order. "No omissions."

"That's right."

"I want you to do whatever you want with me, master," Jerry said. "I'm not trying to be difficult, I just...All I want right now is for my master to want me."

Denton stared down at him for a long time.

No omissions. Jerry cleared his throat. "I'd quite like to come too, master, but I can wait a bit longer for that, if you say that I should."

He stared at Denton's shoulder as he waited for his verdict. For a long time his master stood very still, looking down at him. Finally, Denton reached out to him. He ran his fingertips over his collar. Jerry's own fingers twitched as he fought the urge to reach out and protect the mark.

Denton spotted the move. A moment later, he turned and walked away. He left him there on the bed as he walked out of the room without a word. Straining to hear the sounds of his master walking around the apartment, Jerry tracked his master's progress into the playroom.

Dropping his gaze, Jerry stared down at the blanket. His master had ordered him onto the bed. He was to stay there until he received another order, he knew that. But not rushing after his master right then was just about the hardest thing any dominant had ever asked him to do.

Pulling his knees up in front of him, Jerry wrapped his arms around them and held himself together while he waited for his master to come back to him and tell him everything was okay.

When he returned, Denton was carrying toys. Habit made Jerry looked across at him and try to guess what the other man intended to do with them. Toys meant fun, guessing how they were going to be used on him was all part of the game. But in truth, he didn't really care right then. He turned his full attention back where it belonged — to his master rather than the things he brought into the room with him.

Denton dropped his stash on the bed. He didn't waste any time once his hands were free. Tossing the pillows to one side, he located a strong eyelet they'd screwed in the wall right above the mattress. Denton deftly padlocked one end of a thick chain to the eyelet. He pulled at it, checking the strength. Then he yanked at it again, harder than Jerry would ever be able to. Seemingly satisfied with that end of the chain, he unwound the rest of the length until several yards of chain lay on the bed next to Jerry.

Another padlock was taken from the little pile his master had brought in with him. Denton sat on the mattress next to Jerry. In moments the second padlock linked the other end of the chain to his collar. Denton gave a gentle tug on the chain, just hard enough for Jerry to feel his collar's protection pull against his skin.

"You have free use of the bedroom and the en-suite. If you want to go further than that, you'll have to ask. If I think it's in your best interests to go there, I'll put you on the lead and take you there myself. If I decide you don't need to go anywhere, you'll stay right here."

Jerry nodded.

"You're going to stay very close to your master, where he can keep an eye on you."

He nodded again. "Thank you, master," he whispered.

Denton stroked his hair back from his face and tilted his head back to brush their lips together. "You are mine. You belong to me. Forever. Understand?"

Jerry nodded. Easing out of his panic, he remembered his manners. "May I serve you, master?"

Denton stroked his hair again and slid his hand down Jerry's back so his arm encircled his body. "Since when do you consider having sex with your master a service to perform—a chore to be done?"

Jerry's lips twitched into a smile at the idea. He leaned into his master's touch, nuzzling slightly at his skin. That sort of teasing could always be considered to be blatant permission to play, permission to be silly without worrying his master would take him seriously or think that he wasn't submitting the way he should.

Jerry pressed a kiss onto his master's shoulder, then another one higher up against the ticklish spot on Denton's neck, right on the little patch of skin that could make his master howl with laughter when he got it right.

Denton brushed away another attempt to kiss to that spot, as a reluctant chuckle broke through his struggle to stay serious while he teased. "Brat!"

One push had Jerry flat on his back. A second later Denton had him pinned easily to the mattress. Jerry closed his eyes and took a deep breath, savouring the closeness and the strength of the other man, glorying in his master's love. When he blinked his eyes open, Denton was looking down at him more seriously, studying him for signs of hurt and happiness the way he always did when he was worried about him.

"Let me kiss you, master?" Jerry asked, feeling like a fool for asking, but suddenly realising that was exactly what he needed right then.

Denton let go of one of his wrists and offered his hand to Jerry's lips as if his request made perfect sense. Jerry pressed a kiss against his master's fingers then his palm. He ran his lips over his skin, savouring every taste, like a famished man who'd suddenly stumbled on a feast and couldn't quite believe it was all for him.

His master rolled away from him, letting go of his other wrist as well. Jerry whimpered and followed him. He pressed another kiss to his master's forearm, before quickly brushing another on the inside of his elbow.

"Hush," Denton soothed, tangling one of his hands into Jerry's hair. "There's no rush, pet. Your master's not going anywhere."

Jerry nodded his understanding. He trailed kisses against Denton's skin as his master lay comfortably back on the bed. His lips traced line after line along the older man's muscles, not even seeking out those parts of his master's body that would bring him more pleasure than others.

He brushed his cheek and his forehead against him as he re-explored his lover's skin, just needing the connection, just needing to know he was back with his master. Denton's fingers continued to stroke idly through his hair, keeping them in contact even when Jerry's lips weren't touching him.

He pressed a last kiss against his master's chest and rested his forehead against the other man's ribs.

"Good boy," Denton whispered.

Jerry smiled at the reassurance and pressed an extra kiss against his skin in thanks. Another deep breath and he began to slide his way down his master's body. Just because his master was in a tolerant mood, that didn't give him the right to tease the other man forever.

Denton stopped him short. Jerry glanced up at his master.

"You still need to make your choice, pet."

Jerry frowned. "This was what I wanted, master." His fingers traced the same line along as master's thigh as his kisses had followed.

Denton coaxed him up the bed until they were eyelevel with each other.

"I made my decision weeks ago, Jerry. This is going to happen. All you have to decide is if you want my mouth or if you want to top me properly."

"But you..." he looked down at his master's cock. He was hard and leaking pre-cum after all the kissing and teasing.

"I can wait."

"Will you top me afterwards, master?" Jerry blurted out.

Denton smiled and stroked his cheek as he nodded his agreement. "Make your choice now," he prompted.

Jerry tentatively reached out and touched his master's lips.

Denton nodded his acceptance. He didn't wait around once the choice was made. He easily rolled Jerry onto his back. The friction against Jerry's lips while he kissed his master had all morphed into pleasure as it descended to his cock. He was already achingly hard. Not coming since his master had last topped him pushed him to the edge all too quickly.

There was no teasing. Denton took him straight into his mouth. Jerry gasped and grappled at the sheets as he fought against the very real possibility he would come that first second. Denton hadn't ordered him not to. There would be no punishment if he did. But it would be such a waste.

If his master noticed his struggle against the overload of sensations, it made no difference to his technique. In moments, Jerry was right on the edge of coming again.

Just when he began to tip over the edge, Denton pulled back, letting him slip from between his lips for a moment allowing him to regain control of his body. His lips gentled and caressed his shaft as he bobbed his head lower into Jerry's lap before retreating to tease the glans with his tongue.

Jerry bit his lip and closed his eyes, quickly losing himself in the hot, wet heat that surrounded his shaft, stroking and sucking around him until he was sure his brain would melt.

Denton's grip on his hips tightened. Jerry looked down. His master was looking up at him, studying him intently. Jerry swallowed and licked at his own lips as he gasped for breath. Denton held his gaze as his mouth continued to work his shaft.

Jerry dragged a shaky breath into his lungs. His master lowered his head until the tip of his cock nudged the back of his throat, then he dipped his head further still, until Jerry's cock slipped a little way into the impossibly tight chamber. Denton swallowed, working the muscles around him.

He took him to the edge and backed off. Then he did the same thing again, and again. A blow job that would have satisfied him in seconds, somehow was stretched out and dragged on until Jerry lost all track of just how long Denton's lips teased him. He seemed determined to make it the longest and best blow job Jerry had ever...

Jerry met his master's eyes again. The best blow he'd ever had. A better blow job than anyone else could ever give him — than any woman could ever give him.

Denton seemed to register the fact that Jerry had finally got the point. He could be as bi as he wanted to, as long as he acknowledged that his master was better than any other man or woman on the planet.

Apparently his master was ready to declare himself satisfied with his pet's new level of understanding. He sucked firmly around him. A final flick of his tongue against the most sensitive spot just below the head, and Jerry was finished.

His master kept him in his mouth, sucking around his shaft as he swallowed down his semen, until there was nothing more for him to take. He let Jerry slip from between his lips and stared down at him for several long seconds.

Jerry blinked his eyes open as he finally remembered how to breathe, and why breathing was generally considered important. His whole body seemed to have disintegrated into something so relaxed and sleepy, he could barely raise the energy to keep his eyes open and return his master's gaze. Denton's eyes glittered with success. Jerry smiled.

When Denton leaned over and took a tube of lube from the bedside table, Jerry summoned up the energy to tug at the other man's wrist. Denton turned back to him, looking for an explanation.

"Kiss, master?" Jerry murmured.

Denton smiled and gave him what he wanted, letting him taste the residue of himself in his master's mouth with a slow, deep kiss. Jerry gave a soft, sleepy sigh as his master finally pulled away and nudged him onto his side so he could spoon behind him.

Slicked fingers slid against Jerry's hole. He turned slightly, shifting his legs to give his master better access. Denton pressed a kiss against his shoulder. It didn't take long for Jerry to be ready.

Denton's fingers disappeared. A moment later, the tip of his cock pressed against him. Jerry murmured his pleasure as his master slid inside him. His master had to want to come right away, but he took up a rhythm as slow and sleepy as his submissive felt.

His master pressed another kiss against his shoulder and pushed a little deeper into him. Jerry rocked back against him, letting his master know he didn't have to be so gentle on his account.

Denton put a hand on his hip to still him. "Hush."

Jerry nodded. It was his master's show. He was perfectly free to do whatever he wanted with him. What he seemed to want right then wasn't what Jerry had expected. The need to possess, to mark out his territory didn't seem to be there. Or maybe it was there, just different.

Denton pushed into him again, setting little fireworks off in his prostate with each thrust. Possession—like making sure that Jerry lost any sense of a time when he hadn't lain in his master's arms with his master's shaft buried deep inside him, until Jerry couldn't imagine ever being anywhere else.

It felt like a lifetime later when Denton's hips thrust just that fraction harder, that tiniest bit faster, and his master came inside him. There was a moment when Denton turned away from him to tug the blankets up from the bottom of the bed, but his arms were soon wrapped around him again.

Jerry sighed his sleepy contentment with the world. He shifted as he settled for the night. His fingers brushed against the chain attached to his collar, the metal rattled.

Denton's fingers twined with his, guiding him to hold onto the chain and remember his master's promise, remember that he was safe—back where he belonged. Any tinge of panic that lingered in his mind up until that point disappeared.

"Yours, master," Jerry whispered.

"Yes, pet."

"Always."

"Yes, pet, every bit of you."

Jerry smiled against the pillow, knowing what his master was trying to say without actually blurting it out and being soppy about it. The bit of him that was bi belonged to Denton just as much of every other part of him.

Jerry closed his eyes and let that security wrap tight and perfect around him. "I love you too, master.

THE STROKE OF TWELVE

Dedication

To new years, to new beginnings and to finding new solutions to age old problems.

Chapter One

Wednesday 6th October 2010

"At the stroke of twelve on this day, and on every Wednesday from now on, you will belong to me for one hour. Understand?"

Devon Ashford blinked at the man sitting on the other side of the desk. "What?"

"The appropriate answer is either 'yes, sir' or 'no, sir'," the older man informed him. "Answer the question. Do you understand?"

Devon gave a mental shrug. Okay, so the guy was kinky. He was also as hot as hell. For a man who looked like that, Devon was willing to learn to live with kinky. "Okay."

The guy just stared across the desk at him.

Devon shuffled his trainers on the richly patterned rug. Kinky was fair enough, but standing in front of the big mahogany desk made him feel like he was back in school, in the headmaster's office and waiting to be told how many hours he'd be sent to detention for. He pushed his hand through his hair, shoving the thick blond strands out of his eyes.

Finally, he realised what the other man was waiting for. Devon only just resisted the temptation to roll his eyes. "Yes, sir."

The guy nodded, just once, as if to show he'd heard. That was it.

Devon pushed his hands into his jeans pockets and rocked back on his heels. At any other time, he wouldn't have thought twice about striding quickly around the desk to make his intentions perfectly clear. With any other man, he wouldn't have hesitated to straddle him in his fancy office chair and get the show going. But for some reason he couldn't quite put his finger on, right then and with that man, the idea of assuming the initiative was ludicrous.

Glued to the spot where he'd been ordered to stand, Devon cleared his throat. "So...um..."

The man held up a hand.

Devon watched it for a little while, to see if it was going to do anything interesting, but it just stayed there, indicating he should remain silent.

The big grandfather clock in the hallway outside the office began to chime.

As it slowly tolled the noon hour, Devon studied the older man across the desk. He'd searched the corners of his mind over and over again during the last few days, but all he really remembered was a lot of vodka slammers and, somewhere between late on Saturday night and the early hours of Sunday morning, someone pushing a piece of paper into his hand.

There'd been no name, no number, just a time and an address. This time. This address.

Devon waited out the clock, since it seemed important to the other guy. While it chimed, he happily took the opportunity to study the other man in a way he'd been too drunk to do before.

He was obviously far older than Devon. His hair was dark, but it was already gaining just a touch of grey around his temples. Still, even while he was sitting behind the desk, it was clear that the other man was also much taller and broader across the shoulders than he was.

Devon wasn't going to complain about that. Stern lips, brooding brown eyes, square jaw...Devon quietly nodded to himself. The guy was definitely worth putting up with a bit of leather for.

As the last note from the clock's chimes faded from the air, he opened his mouth to ask exactly what the other guy was into.

The older man cut him off before he could utter a single syllable.

"Strip."

Devon forced out a slightly nervous laugh. "You don't waste any time once you get going, do you?"

The guy didn't so much as crack a smile.

"Don't I even get some music to strip to?" Devon joked, but even he couldn't manage to chuckle this time. Suddenly uncertain for no logical reason, he pushed his hands deeper into his pockets.

"Don't dance," the man told him. "Don't perform. If I want you to put on a show, I'll tell you. Just take your clothes off." His voice matched everything else about him perfectly, deep and rich and apparently created especially for giving orders.

Devon took his hands out of his pockets. He pushed one hand through his hair again, shoving the scruffy blond stands out of his eyes as he considered his options. It wasn't as if either of them thought they were hooking up for anything but a midday quickie. They'd obviously be getting naked at some point, but still...

Thrusting his nerves aside, Devon grabbed the neck of his T-shirt and pulled it over his head. Dropping it to the floor at his feet, he glanced across the desk again. The man said nothing. Realising that going slowly from that point on would only make him more anxious, Devon kicked off his trainers. Quickly tugging off his socks, he tossed them on the pile. That only left his jeans and his boxers. Unbuttoning his fly, he pushed them down together and quickly stepped out of the tangled mess of denim and cotton.

Suddenly, all the confidence Devon had acquired since he'd turned eighteen, come out, and discovered that most guys really liked the way he looked — dressed or undressed — drained away. He didn't get the feeling the guy watching him was easily impressed by anything, not even a naked and willing twenty-three year old.

"Pick up your clothes, fold them neatly and place them on the table."

Devon glanced at the side table the other man nodded towards. He looked back to the guy. He was serious...he was bloody well serious!

Devon frowned. Hell, even if he wasn't delighted with what had rolled up onto his doorstep, it was just basic good manners for him to say something complimentary to the guy standing stark bollock naked in front of him.

Not knowing what else to do, something inside Devon latched on to the older man's order. Bending down, he picked up his clothes and carried them over to the side table. Quickly folding them up, he set them in a lopsided little pile before glancing over his shoulder.

"Back where you were," the older man ordered.

Devon returned to the spot where he'd originally been told to stand — right in the middle of the rug, facing the desk.

The man studied him vigilantly for several minutes. There was nothing particularly sinister or even licentious about his gaze. He looked remarkably detached, completely composed, like a scientist examining some damn bug under a microscope.

Devon's hands clenched into fists at his sides as he fought against a new-found instinct to blush and cover up his rapidly hardening cock. "You know, if you just wanted to look at a naked man, there are websites you could have gone to and saved me the taxi fare out here."

"Turn around."

Devon sighed. His clothes were already on the other side of the room. Since he was already pretty damn committed to whatever game the guy was choreographing, he figured he might as well play along and do as he was told for a little while longer — if only out of a morbid curiosity as to what would happen next.

He turned his back on the other man, but looked over his shoulder just a second later. "You never did tell me your name."

"You may address me as sir."

Turning back to him, Devon frowned, pale blond eyebrows coming together behind the long blond fringe. "You're serious," he realised.

"Perfectly." At long last, the other man stood up and walked around the table to greet him. "For the next hour, you belong to me. You'll do exactly as you're told, without exception."

Devon stayed rooted to the spot, watching him come closer, step by step.

"If I give you an order you understand, you'll say, 'yes, sir'. If I give you an order you don't understand you'll say 'I don't understand, sir'."

The older man stopped and waited.

Devon tilted his head back and looked up at him. Damn, but he was a hell of a lot taller than he remembered him being through the haze of vodka. "Yes, sir," he said, for lack of any other words in his head right then.

"Your name?" the older man prompted as he stepped between Devon and the high window on the other side of the desk. He was a good few inches broader than Devon remembered, too. His shadow seemed to reach for miles.

He blinked up at the other guy. Name. Yes. He had one of those. "Everyone calls me Sparks."

Not even a flicker of a smile. "Is that what's written on your birth certificate?"

Devon cleared his throat. "Devon Ashford. Ash, fire, sparks...um...yeah..."

If he got the play on words, the larger man didn't seem particularly impressed by it.

"You're not into anything really hardcore, are you?" Devon blurted out.

Without bothering to answer, the guy reached for his face and caught his chin between his thumb and forefinger. Firmly tilting his head back, he studied Devon for a long time, turning his face this way and that as if to catch the different angles of the light that flooded in through another window on the adjacent side of the room.

He ran his fingers over Devon's cheeks, where he hadn't bothered to shave the previous day's stubble away. His fingertips caressed the dark shadows under his eyes.

"You don't talk much, do you?" Devon said, desperately trying not to sound too nervous and failing miserably.

The guy turned his attention to Devon's hair. He ran his fingers through it as if studying the texture and debating if it was an acceptable standard.

"You're not part of that white slave thing they're on about on the news, are you?" Devon quipped.

Completely ignoring every sodding word, the older man ran his hands down Devon's throat, examining the skin there too. He had huge hands. They could easily span his neck.

Devon closed his eyes. Strangulation had to be a pretty painful way to go. It probably wasn't the most painful way though.

"What do you think is the most painful way to die?" Devon asked at random, unable to bear the silence in the room a moment longer.

The other man looked down at him, straight into his eyes. "I have no interest in killing you. You'd be no use to me dead."

"So, you do want to screw me then?" Devon asked, hopefully. Whatever he was into, something which actually involved sex had to make a damn sight more sense than anything that had happened since he'd walked into the office.

The man offered no response as his inspection moved on to Devon's shoulders.

"Raise your arms, extend them in a straight line to either side of your body, palms up."

Devon hesitated, but he'd put up with this much weirdness, he didn't really seem to have anything to lose by putting his arms out too.

Each limb was inspected individually. Long, strong fingers kneaded into the muscles all the way down his arms, not missing one single inch of skin along the way.

The inspection focussed around the veins inside his elbows for a long time. "I'm not using, if that's what you want to know," Devon said. "I don't do drugs—never have."

His words didn't make one jot of difference to anything.

Devon closed his eyes. In spite of all sense or reason, each strong, impersonal touch was going straight to his cock, making him harden a little more quickly with each moment that passed.

When Devon opened his eyes, he looked up, trying to read the other man's emotions. He didn't have much expression at all. He just seemed completely focussed on his task.

Devon tried to remember a time when anyone had ever looked at him that way, but he was sure no one ever had. Guys looked. But that was just a 'you're pretty, want to screw?' sort of looking. It was never like this.

Since the man seemed to be finished with whatever he'd wanted to do with his arms, Devon lowered them back to his sides, surprised how quickly his shoulders had started to feel sore just from holding that one position.

"I didn't tell you to move. Put your arms back where they were."

Their eyes met. Devon thought about telling the man to sod off and stop playing silly buggers, but, for some reason, the words just didn't come. He put his arms out to the sides once more, palms up, exposing his torso and practically inviting the man to continue his examination.

Devon nibbled on his bottom lip as the other man's hands made their way down his chest until they paused for several minutes to tease his nipples. Devon had never thought them particularly sensitive before. After thirty seconds with this guy tweaking and examining the little nubs of nerve ending, he was reasonably sure he could come just from that. He breathed a deep sigh of relief when the guy's inspection dropped lower without actually lingering long enough to tip him over the edge.

His abs were studied one by one. Devon instinctively tensed the muscles, trying to make his build appear to its best advantage. Even through the black suit he wore, Devon could tell the older man was far more heavily muscled than him.

The younger man shifted a little uncomfortably under the comparison. "I keep meaning to spend more time in the gym." He failed to be at all surprised when the older man ignored his latest attempt at conversation.

It wasn't as if the guy could miss the fact that Devon's cock was as hard as a rock. But he didn't make any comment on that as he trailed his fingers over his skin and reached the last of his stomach muscles. He skipped over his crotch altogether and dropped his assessment to Devon's legs.

As he watched the older man go over every inch of him, right down to the gaps between his toes and to lifting up each foot so he could examine the sole, Devon tried to think of something appropriate to say. Right then, he'd have settled for any words that broke the silence, but his mouth was dry and his mind blank. All he could think about was those hands inspecting him and that at the end of all this, that the guy would inevitably pass some sort of verdict on everything he'd seen.

Finished with his legs, the man stepped behind him. "Feet shoulder width apart, bend over and put your hands on your knees."

Devon looked over his shoulder. Something in the back of his mind kept whispering to him, telling him that he really didn't have to do what this guy told him to. The other man didn't have any right to order him around or expect his obedience.

The sensible little voice was impatiently overruled by the part of him which screamed its desire to know what happened next—the same part that yelled out a reminder that his cock was hard and curving up towards his stomach. He might still get laid if he stuck around and played the game for just a little while longer.

Devon shuffled his feet apart and bent over, arching his back slightly to present his arse in the best possible manner.

Hands massaged his buttocks, kneading the firm muscles in a strong, confident grip. One hand moved to the small of his back and steadied him. The other disappeared for a moment, to come back, slicked, to press against his hole.

Devon tensed as the fingers teased against him, testing the ring of muscle to gauge how tight he was. It was stupid to be self conscious at the intimacy of it. It wasn't as if no guy had ever touched him before—as if dozens of men hadn't done the same at one time or another. Although, as the inspection slowly progressed, Devon couldn't deny just how different this was to anything he'd ever done with anyone else.

The guy's fingers finally slid inside him. Biting his lip, Devon tried to stay silent as they worked their way deeper into his arse, but the moment they found his prostate, he whimpered and instinctively tried to push back.

"Stay still, Devon. If I want you to move, I'll tell you to." The guy really did possess a magnificent voice, so low and stern. He sounded so serious about everything he said and so damn sure Devon would want to do as he commanded.

And he did try to do as the other man said, he tried like hell. But if the guy truly wanted him to stay still, he really needed to stop rubbing against his prostate that way. Devon murmured his approval, low in his throat as the fingers worked him to fever pitch. Just when it was starting to be enough, just as Devon thought he might actually be able to come from that alone, and just as he decided that would be a really great thing to be able to do right then, the fingers disappeared from his world.

"Stand up straight. Hands behind your back," the guy snapped.

Devon, his breath coming in rapid, frustrated gasps, straightened up and looked over his shoulder. "Okay," he managed to say, reasonably calmly. "Kinky is fair enough but..." He trailed off as their eyes met.

The man held his gaze until Devon, of all the stupid things to do, blushed. Dropping his gaze, and desperate to do something to ease his confusion, he latched on to the other man's order once more, put his hands behind his back and wrapped one hand around the other wrist to keep them in place.

A warm, strong hand reached out and palmed his testicles, rolling the tight sac within its grasp and examining it for several minutes. Devon bit his lip. He tried as hard as he knew how to stay still and quiet and allow the man do whatever he wanted with him.

In a way he didn't understand, he really wanted the man to approve of him — to realise he was doing his very best to follow his orders. A few whimpers of frustration and moans of appreciation made it past his lips despite his best attempts, but the older man made no comment on them.

When his hand finally wrapped around Devon's erection, the younger man almost dropped to his knees, half in grateful thanks and half because his legs suddenly decided they didn't want to support him anymore.

Keeping him in hand, the larger man stepped behind Devon and allowed him to lean back against his body. He did so, grateful for anything that might keep him on his feet and his cock at the right height to keep receiving that touch.

The older man's other hand steadied him at the waist as the fingers wrapped around his cock stroked him and toyed with him, pushing him close to the edge before pulling him back from the brink to try something else. Whenever he had Devon mere milliseconds away from coming, the guy stopped again. More and more pleasure rushed through the younger man's body, until his head spun with it and the only thing keeping him upright was the guy giving all the orders.

Devon's hands twitched between them, trapped between their bodies, unable to reach out and explore in return, unable to offer the other man anything but their obedience as they remained where the older man had ordered them to be.

Devon wasn't sure at what exact point he started to hold back, unsure if he was allowed to come regardless of how much he wanted to. Still, clinging to his self control only did him so much good once the older man finally settled on a rhythm he seemed willing to like for more than a few consecutive seconds.

Unable to do anything else, Devon thrust into the tight grip and came into the relative stranger's hand. The older man stroked him all the way through his orgasm as Devon pressed back against him, half collapsing against the more muscular frame.

Finally the other man's hand stilled.

As Devon's breathing evened out a little and he started to be able to think of something other than his own cock, he realised he could feel the other guy's erection digging into him, just to one side of where his hands crossed behind his back. He tried to bring his mind back together and focus on what that meant.

The moment he straightened up and took all his own weight back onto his feet, the guy stepped away from him. Devon tried not to regret the loss as cold air replaced the warmth of another man's body.

"That was..." Devon trailed off. Bizarre was what it was. The fact it was strangely erotic didn't change the fact it was still very, *very* strange. Not sure he'd like the answer, he found himself asking anyway. "What do you want me to do for you?"

The older man walked calmly back to the other side of the desk. Devon took a step forwards, guessing he was going to be on his knees in front of the guy's chair at any moment.

"Next Wednesday, your hour will start at twelve o'clock exactly. The door will be unlocked at five minutes to the hour. I don't tolerate tardiness. Close the door behind you on the way out."

"What?" Devon blinked at him. In the background he could hear the faint sound of the grandfather clock starting to strike the hour once more. "That's it? You just..."

The man stared across at him, not one hint of frustration visible in his expression.

Devon frowned as he dropped his gaze, wondering if he'd done something to suddenly put the man off. By the time he looked up, the man had turned his attention to the paperwork spread out across his desk.

Devon stood naked in the middle of the man's office for several minutes, watching him go through the files.

He had to say something, the only question was what. "You're sure you don't want to do anything else?"

The other man looked up. "When I want something, I'll tell you."

A few more minutes passed. Devon slowly walked across to his clothes and scrambled into them. His fingers shook slightly as he shoved his feet into his trainers. He glanced back to the man behind the desk as he made his way out of the room, but right then he didn't know what else to do except follow the last order the man had given him.

He closed the door behind him on the way out.

* * * *

Wednesday 13th January 2010

Devon pushed back his sleeve and glanced at his watch. Pushing his hands deeper into his coat pockets he walked a little faster. Turning the corner into a quiet side street in the oldest part of town, he walked swiftly up the drive leading to the offices of Templeton, Crawford and Associates.

"You're an idiot, Devon," he whispered under his breath. There was no doubt about that fact in his mind. Only a complete pillock would put up with all the bull he'd gone through the previous Wednesday, then go back for more a week later.

Reaching the front door, he attempted to turn the old-fashioned brass handle. It wouldn't budge. Devon gave the door a gentle shove with his shoulder. Nothing.

Frowning at the black painted woodwork, he looked at his wristwatch again. It was already a few minutes past twelve. If the man was going to insist on stopping at one o'clock again, then their time together was rapidly running out.

Devon reached for the doorbell. The guy had probably just forgotten to unlock it. The faint sound of the bell ringing inside made it through the door. Rocking on his heels, he waited for someone to answer it. After a few minutes he glared at the bell and rang it again.

Maybe the older man had forgotten about their appointment. Devon's teeth nipped worriedly into his bottom lip. He may have only known the guy for an hour, but he was already sure he wasn't the type to forget things. Taking a few steps back, Devon peeked around the side of the building. A path led towards the back of the offices. He followed it around until he reached a window that looked into the same room he'd spent an hour in a week earlier.

Gazing through the glass, Devon's gaze fell on the same guy sitting at the same desk he'd been fantasising about being screwed across all week. He watched the...the dominant he supposed he was, through the window for a few seconds before tapping on the glass.

There was no way the guy didn't hear the light rap on the pane, but all he did was glance once at his wristwatch and turn his attention back to his paperwork.

Just because he was a few minutes late?

Devon stared silently through the window. He was a few minutes late and the guy wasn't even going to let him into the building? That was...

Gritting his teeth, Devon spun around and stormed away from the window. He kept going, around the office, down the drive and along the street. At the far end of the road, he stopped and looked back for a moment.

Shaking his head, he turned away once more. This time, he kept going.

He wasn't going to be treated like that. If the guy was that petty he could find some other idiot to play stupid games with.

Mr. Andrew Templeton kept his eyes fixed firmly on his paperwork, until he could be sure the boy was completely out of sight of the window. When he finally looked up, he gazed through the glass without really seeing anything that was on the other side of it.

If Devon was anything like the man Templeton thought he might be, if the potential he saw in the younger man really did exist, he'd be back. And if he didn't come back...

Holding back a sigh, Templeton turned his attention back to his work. If Devon didn't come back, there was little he could do about it. It was impossible for anyone to fulfil a need that didn't actually exist in a man.

Chapter Two

Wednesday 20th January 2010

Devon glanced at his watch yet again. His arm was starting to get tired from him lifting it to look at the damn thing so often.

Ten minutes seemed to be a good compromise. If he turned up more than ten minutes early, he'd look pathetic. He shuffled his feet on the slightly uneven pavement while he waited at the end of the road until the longest hand moved just a little further around the dial.

Arriving more than ten minutes early would imply he didn't have anything else to do with his time. It might be true, but he didn't need to bloody well advertise the fact. Nor did he need to make it completely obvious that he'd been thinking about the guy almost non-stop for the last fortnight. There was no need for him to shout out just how much he hoped that he hadn't screwed up whatever the hell it was that might happen between them on Wednesdays at noon.

Fifteen minutes would be desperate. Five would imply he was unrepentant. Ten minutes said, sorry I was late last time—let's put that behind us and have sex.

Exactly ten minutes before noon, Devon stood outside the front door to Templeton, Crawford and Associates. The guy had said he'd open it at five minutes to the hour. He hadn't said knock, or ring, or walk around the back. Devon had run everything the other man had said to him over and over in his head for fourteen days. He was pretty sure the guy was the type to be very specific in his orders.

At exactly five minutes to the hour, the sound of a key being turned in the lock floated through from the other side of the door. When the glossy black surface didn't move and the door failed to swing open on its own, Devon risked a tiny bit of initiative.

He turned the handle and peeked into the hallway.

No one was there, but the door leading into the office was open. Devon walked in and stood in front of the desk, just as he'd been ordered to once before.

The older man looked up.

Devon cleared his throat. "I'm sorry I was late last time." He was sure he hadn't intended any other words to attach themselves onto the end of the sentence, but one did. "Sir."

The dominant nodded, just once, and went back to his paperwork.

Devon waited and tried not to fidget.

Eventually, the clock began to strike the hour. The other man stood up and walked around the desk to face Devon.

"At the stroke of twelve on this day and on every Wednesday from now on, you belong to me for one hour. Understand?"

"Yes, sir."

"There are to be no repeats of last week's mistake," he went on.

"No, sir," Devon agreed quickly.

"Very well then. Strip."

Devon took off his clothes without wasting any time. Eager to show how much he'd learnt from his last visit, he folded his clothes as neatly as he knew how, and placed them on the side table. Then he returned to the spot where he'd stood before.

He looked to the other man in the hope of approval and received another nod. The guy walked slowly around him, studying him with no less intensity than on his previous visit.

"Am I allowed to ask you a question, sir?"

"If you want to ask me something, the correct form is, 'may I know', followed by whatever it is you wish to query. Asking if you can ask something is contradictory."

"May I know if you are Templeton, Crawford or Associates, sir?"

"For what purpose?" The older man idly trailed a line down the centre of Devon's back with his fingertips as he spoke.

"I..." Devon stalled as one finger traced further down the crease between his buttocks. He took a deep breath and tried again. "I'd like to know your name, sir."

"That's important to you?"

Devon closed his eyes and tried to stay still as the fingertip's touch reached the top of his spine before beginning to descend again.

"Yes, sir."

"Would I be the first man you've had sex with without knowing his name?"

Unable to work out what the right answer would be, Devon had little choice but to opt for the truth. "No, sir, you wouldn't be the first."

"Then why does it matter?"

Words rushed to the tip of Devon's tongue, but he bit them back. It mattered because *he* mattered, because the hour he'd spent in that office two weeks earlier was different to any other hour he'd ever spent with anyone else. "You're different, sir," he finally whispered.

"Mr. Templeton," the other man said from behind him, as his finger trailed down Devon's spine once more.

"Thank you, sir." It was astonishing how easily the honorific slipped from between his lips now, how instinctive it seemed to be. Still, as natural as everything felt between them, Devon had given himself a stern talking to since last time. "May I also know if you intend to give me a safe word, sir?"

"If you want to say no, say no. If you want to leave, say so and I won't try to stop you. You don't need a safe word."

Devon nodded, suddenly embarrassed he'd ever asked for such a thing. "Yes, sir."

Mr. Templeton's fingertips left him as he walked around to face Devon and made him look up. "If the question was inappropriate, I'd have told you so."

Devon nodded again.

"Bend over that desk, legs apart, hands behind your back. Make yourself as comfortable as you can. You'll be there until the end of the hour."

Devon looked to the desk the other man indicated. There were so many different things he felt like he should ask, but the words wouldn't come to his lips right then. Mr. Templeton had told him what to do. In some way it felt as if that was all he really needed to know.

Stepping up to the edge of a smaller mahogany desk on the opposite side of the room, Devon bent over it, settling himself quickly against the green leather inlayed into the surface. He was already more than half hard. With his cock trapped between the desk and his body, every movement he made as he spread his legs and placed his hands behind his back sent a peak of pleasure rushing to his shaft and made him stiffen further.

Devon closed his eyes and took a deep breath as he rested his cheek on the desk top. They were just going to have sex. There was nothing scary about that. There was no reason to be worried.

None of those facts stopped his nerves from doubling over and over again while Mr. Templeton left him there, waiting, with no control over what would happen next.

With his head lowered to rest on the leather, it was impossible for Devon to see what was happening behind him. He could hear Mr. Templeton moving about, but the sounds meant nothing to him in the unfamiliar room. A scrape of wood against wood could have been a drawer being pulled out. Or it could have been a chair being dragged against the floor. Hell, for all Devon knew the guy had set up a damn woodworking shop on the other side of the office.

Lost in his own thoughts, Devon yelped as a large, strong hand came to rest on his shoulder.

"Sorry, sir." Heat rushed to his cheeks at the silly mistake.

Mr. Templeton didn't say a single word in response. He just stroked his hand down Devon's body, the flat of his palm hot and solid against his bare skin. The touch soothed something inside Devon as he lay over the desk, telling him that everything was under the older man's control, that he didn't have to worry about anything but doing as he was told — and that it was a good thing.

The dominant's other hand slipped between Devon's buttocks and started to play with his hole as his fingers deftly prepared him. Slick digits slid into Devon again and again until the tight ring of muscle relaxed and welcomed the intrusion, eager for every caress.

Behind his back, Devon's own hands grasped at thin air, desperate to reach out for the other man but sure that no such touch would be welcomed. Without even being told, he knew that would be a privilege he'd have to earn. He squirmed against the table, rubbing his cheek against the leather beneath him as pleasure built up inside him and he realised he had no way to release it.

The older man's fingers slid out of him, leaving him empty and impatient. Devon was half sure it was all a bloody tease again. Then he heard a condom wrapper tear. A moment later, the blunt pressure of an erection pressed against his hole.

Placing his hand on Devon's shoulder once more, Mr. Templeton steadied him as he pushed into him very slowly, obviously making damn sure he felt every inch of his long, hard shaft sliding into him, stretching him wide open and filling him perfectly.

As he felt Mr. Templeton's hips settle against his buttocks, Devon let out a contented little sigh against the leather-topped desk. Somehow the older man kept his rhythm incredibly slow, impossibly steady as he pulled back and thrust into him again and again.

Devon bit down hard on his lip, desperately trying not to ask for more, no matter how much he wanted it.

Eventually, the build up of pure pleasure was more than he could take. It became a choice between speaking or moving without permission. "Please, sir," he whispered, hoping like hell he was picking the lesser of two evils.

The dominant made no response. He changed nothing about his deep, determined thrusts.

Devon whimpered his frustration as his hands fisted behind his back and his fingernails bit into his palms.

Very gradually, someone, somewhere answered Devon's prayers. The older man's rhythm started to speed up. Stroke by stroke he started to push into him harder and faster, rubbing the length of his shaft against his prostate on every movement, making him whimper and squirm as far as the other man's grip would allow.

The faster thrusts rocked him against the desk, rubbing his cock against the wood and leather. Devon's breaths sped up, his pulse raced, his cock screamed for release. As frantically as he tried to hold back, Devon's will cracked under the onslaught of sensations. He jerked under Mr. Templeton's hands and came, semen spreading beneath him, coating his stomach and the leather beneath him as his hips pumped against the hard edge of the desk.

Mr. Templeton thrust into him all the way through his orgasm, not even faltering as Devon's hole clenched and relaxed helplessly around the other man's shaft. Some minutes later, as Devon lay across the table, trying desperately to catch his breath and order his scattered thoughts, he felt Mr. Templeton come inside him.

A steadying grip on his shoulder, and the other on his hip, tightened for a moment as Mr. Templeton buried himself as far as he could inside Devon with one final harsh thrust, then fell still, with barely a sound.

A minute passed and he pulled away. Devon stayed where he was, grateful for a few extra moments of rest before he had to get up and try to make his brain work. He listened to the sound of Mr. Templeton dispensing with the used condom and straightening his clothes with an almost otherworldly sense of calm, and waited patiently for the order to move.

The command didn't come.

The sound of the older man moving around the room behind him floated across to Devon, but there were no words. Then complete silence fell. He started to wonder if he was alone in the room, if Mr. Templeton had just walked away and left him to be discovered by the first secretary to return from her lunch break. His heartbeat began to speed up as he wished like hell that he'd rested his other cheek on the desk and given himself a better view of the room.

The first indication that someone was still there was a sudden firm pressure against his hole. Devon tensed. It hadn't been that long. He was still soft. There was no way in hell Mr. Templeton should be ready for another round.

A hand settled in the small of his back, as if in silent reassurance. Devon glanced behind him as well as he could from his position, but he knew who he'd see there. Even after such a short acquaintance, he'd know his touch anywhere.

The pressure against his hole increased until something slid slickly inside him. A butt plug. Devon relaxed a little. Barely a moment later, he tensed all over again, as it started to vibrate, sending a shiver through his spine and coursing out into every bit of his body. Mr. Templeton pressed against the base of the plug, jostling it inside him as he adjusted the setting. It whirled away faster. Devon bit his lip as he heard the dominant walk away.

A few seconds later, paper rustled. Devon closed his eyes as the vibrations continued to purr away inside him and coaxed him to slowly harden against the sticky table while the other man calmly went back to work.

He desperately wanted to move, to ease the soreness in his joints and work out the tension building in his muscles, but he found himself waiting for permission, waiting for an order from Mr. Templeton before he could do anything at all.

The room remained silent except for paper moving against paper or the occasional flurry of clicking keys on a keyboard, and Devon stayed where he was, listening to Mr. Templeton work. He'd almost forgotten there was a world outside the room when he suddenly heard the clock in the hallway begin to chime in the next hour.

"You may rise and get dressed," Mr. Templeton said when the clock had finished its proclamation.

Devon obediently began to lift himself away from the table. Every muscle in his body ached from maintaining that position, but, for some stupid reason, he found himself trying to hide the fact as best he could. A few stiff muscles weren't as important as the older man's approval. The last thing he wanted was for Mr. Templeton to think he couldn't hack whatever game it was they were playing together.

Devon straightened up and brought his arms back in front of him. Pain flared along his shoulders. Already hard again, he wasn't entirely sure if he should try to hide that fact too, or if Mr. Templeton would be pleased that the vibrations of the plug made him bounce back so quickly.

He hesitated for a moment, wondering if Mr. Templeton expected him to remove the plug before he left. But, since no mention was made of it, he could only assume he was supposed to keep it in place, still purring away inside him, when he left—a little reminder of the hour they'd spent together.

Devon slowly put his clothes back on. Every movement made the plug shift inside him and tease him. Devon closed his eyes as he wondered how long it would keep purring away for before the batteries finally ran out. Something told him that no matter how long it took, he wouldn't take it out until they did.

A glance back to the little desk he'd bent over showed where he'd left his mark on the surface.

Cleaning it up as well as he could with tissues from his jeans pockets, for the first time in his life Devon did his best to leave a room as neat and tidy as he'd found it. When he was done, he finally found the courage to turn around and meet Mr. Templeton's gaze across the room.

The older man was leaning back in his chair with his fingers steepled in front of him, watching every move he made.

Devon cleared his throat. He was supposed to go now, he knew that. He'd been given an order, he was expected to obey it. He walked across to the door and turned the handle. At the last minute he stopped.

"Thank you, sir," he offered.

Mr. Templeton nodded, just once. Devon liked to think he saw a tiny spark of approval in the gesture.

* * * *

Wednesday 27th January 2010

"At the stroke of twelve on this day and on every weekday from now on, you will belong to me for one hour. Do you understand?"

"Every weekday?" Devon echoed.

Mr. Templeton held his gaze for several seconds. "Is that a problem?"

Devon shook his head. "No, sir." His life already revolved around Wednesdays at noon.

Every other moment, he either found himself remembering the last hour he'd been permitted to spend in the older man's office, or looking forward to his next visit there, or just thinking about Mr. Templeton in general.

The idea of actually being allowed to visit him five days a week wasn't just not a problem, it was bloody amazing.

Devon frowned as he analysed what he'd actually said in response to the announcement. "I mean, 'yes, sir', to every day. And 'no, sir', to it being a problem." He mentally rolled his eyes at himself. It was obviously a very good thing Mr. Templeton rarely initiated conversations with him if this was the amount of sense he made when he tried to answer a simple sodding question.

The dominant said nothing. He walked back to his desk and sat down behind the huge expanse of mahogany. "Take off your clothes, then come here, Devon."

Quickly slipping out of his jeans and shirt, Devon put them neatly on the side table and walked back to what he was quickly starting to think of as 'his spot' in front of the desk.

"Here," Mr. Templeton corrected. Swivelling his chair to one side and tapping the rug to one side of his chair with the toe of his shoe.

Devon hurried around and stood where he was directed. "Kneel."

He knelt and was immediately reassured to know he wasn't the only one sporting a hard-on. Even if Mr. Templeton was still fully clothed, his erection was tenting his trousers and Devon had the perfect point of view.

The chair spun back to face the desk and Mr. Templeton turned his attention to his paperwork, seeming to forget there was a naked submissive at his side for several long minutes.

Devon knelt there, silently watching him work, waiting as patiently as he could for any command the dominant cared to offer him.

"In the cabinet on the left hand side of that window there's a file marked 'Southwark project'. Find it and bring it back to me."

It wasn't quite the order Devon had been looking forward to. He was there to screw, not to play the errand boy.

When he didn't immediately jump to obey, Mr. Templeton glanced towards him. "Did you understand the order, Devon?"

Devon looked down in confusion. "Yes, sir…" A glance up, and he saw how carefully the older man was watching him.

The order was a test. And he was failing it. Perhaps it was too late to make a really good impression, but Devon quickly got to his feet. He found the file and brought it back. Mr. Templeton took it from him as Devon knelt next to his chair once more. The older man stuck a little sticky arrow on the edge of one of the pages, then he handed both the little pad of sticky arrows and the file back to Devon.

"Mark each point where it requires a signature."

Devon frowned, but he took what was offered to him and did as he was told. His task completed, he waited for Mr. Templeton to glance in his direction, and offered him the completed file.

The dominant took it back and absentmindedly stroked his fingers through Devon's hair in quiet praise.

Heat raced to the younger man's cheeks, not so much because Mr. Templeton had just patted him on the head for being a good boy, but because Devon was sure a grown man really shouldn't like that gesture as much as he did. Even so, hot on the heels of embarrassment was the desire to know how he could keep the other man happy with him.

To his surprise, it wasn't hard. Mr. Templeton seemed more than willing to provide him with several other little jobs. And each completed task earned the same reward – a gentle touch and a moment in which to bask in the dominant's approval. Both rewards were addictive. Devon quickly found himself watching the older man for any sign that there was something, anything, he could do to serve him.

When Mr. Templeton set aside another file and turned his chair towards Devon again, he expected another little order to be issued, but the older man just gazed down at him, studying him in silence for several minutes.

Devon looked to the floor. Mr. Templeton's shoes were really shiny. There were even little reflections visible in the highly polished surfaces.

"Look up."

Devon glanced up and met Mr. Templeton's gaze.

The dominant reached out and traced a line around Devon's lips with the tip of his finger. The skin he caressed tingled under his touch. Devon's eyes immediately dropped to the older man's fly, before he recalled his last command and dragged his gaze back up.

Mr. Templeton actually half-smiled at him. "That's right, Devon," he said, in the same perfectly calm and incredibly serious tone of voice he always used. "I'm going to tell you to suck my cock."

Devon nodded enthusiastically. "Yes, sir."

Mr. Templeton leant back in his chair. He nodded once.

Rising on his knees, Devon stopped sitting comfortably back on his heels and reached for the dominant's belt.

Deftly freeing him from his clothes, Devon risked another glance up at Mr. Templeton's face.

"May I know what you like, sir?" The words came out far more softly than he intended.

The older man touched his cheek and made him look up when he'd have dropped his gaze. "Are you telling me that you've so little experience you need to ask?"

Devon shook his head. "No, sir. I know what I'm doing. I just thought, if there's something you particularly..." He trailed off. The only words inside his head were the truth, and he couldn't bring himself to utter them.

He really didn't want to screw this up.

"It's not a test. If I want you to do something specific I'll tell you."

"Yes, sir."

Leaning in, Devon carefully wrapped his lips around the tip of the dominant's cock. Steadying the length with his fist, he lapped at the head. This had to be good for his...with any other man he'd have said his lover. But, even as he knelt there, Devon knew that it would have been the wrong word for what they had together.

He wasn't an idiot. He had the internet. He'd seen the porn and surfed the kinky toy shops often enough.

Mr. Templeton was his master.

Dipping his head to take the other man's cock deeper into his mouth, it was the word and not what he was doing that made him suddenly blush bright red. Sucking gently around the dominant's shaft, pulling back to tease the tip with his tongue, Devon realised for the first time that he was kneeling at his master's feet.

A shot of panic raced through him at the unfamiliar thought. He sucked harder. Extending his mouth with his fist so the whole shaft was covered, Devon started to speed up his movements, working on autopilot.

"More slowly, Devon. Concentrate on the head."

A glance up, and the younger man tried to signal he'd heard and understood with his eyes, unwilling to let his master's cock slip from between his lips to answer right then.

As he altered his technique, Mr. Templeton reached out stroked his cheek. It felt like praise — like Mr. Templeton was pleased with his efforts, even though he wasn't getting the perfect blow job Devon had hoped to provide.

Slowly, pre-cum began to leak onto his tongue. The older man's taste filled his mouth. Second-hand pleasure rushed through Devon's veins. He brought his other hand up to rest against the base of his master's cock. It was the only way he could be sure his fingers wouldn't stray towards his own aching shaft as he felt a drop of his own pre-cum trail down the underside of his erection.

He whimpered around the dominant's cock, but he kept his hands up, kept his focus on the other man's pleasure rather than his own.

Guided onward by occasional instructions and corrections from above, Devon slowly brought the other man to the edge of his orgasm. The older man's hand tightened around the padded arm of his chair. His muscles tensed. His feet pressed down against the floor to either side of Devon's knees. One tiny little gasp of pleasure escaped from between the dominant's lips.

Mr. Templeton's hips rocked forward as he came in Devon's mouth. Quickly swallowing it down, the younger man savoured the salt as it slid over his tongue and relished the success of knowing he'd given the dominant satisfaction.

As the older man's cock slowly softened in his mouth, Devon remained exactly where he was. Until he was ordered to move, he was going to stay precisely where he wanted to be and cherish every damn moment of it.

Eventually, he was forced to give up his prize as Mr. Templeton calmly retrieved his cock from his mouth and tucked himself away. But the dominant didn't immediately send him away.

"Tell me, what made you blush?"

Devon gave him his best blankly innocent look.

Mr. Templeton raised his eyebrow, obviously not in the least impressed.

"I..." Devon searched for the right words. "Sir, are you my master?" he blurted out.

The dominant didn't seem the least shocked by the question. He stroked Devon's cheek in a mildly approving gesture. "Between twelve and one on weekdays, yes, I'm your master."

Devon nodded. "Thank you, sir."

Barely a moment passed before the clock began to strike one. They stayed where they were, with Mr. Templeton's finger still gently caressing Devon's cheek, until the last chime sounded.

His master took his touch away then, and nodded for Devon to get dressed. Devon did so, carefully covering up his own, untended erection as he buttoned his fly.

At the door leading back into the hall, he paused on the threshold.

"Tomorrow, sir?" he checked.

"Yes, tomorrow is a week day," Mr. Templeton agreed.

Devon nodded. "Yes, sir."

* * * *

Thursday 11th February 2010

By ten minutes to twelve, Devon was shivering. He wrapped his arms more tightly around his body as he stamped his feet in a last ditch effort to keep the blood pushing through his veins. The cold spell they'd been predicting really had to pick *today* to kick in with a bang.

Every movement made his head pound all the worse. He swallowed down his queasiness and wrapped his arms even tighter around his T-shirt covered torso.

At five minutes to twelve, right on time, Mr. Templeton unlocked the outer door and let him into the building. Devon shuffled into the office. Just like any other weekday, he went to his spot on the rug in front of the desk, but Mr. Templeton didn't retrace his steps back to sit behind his desk the way he usually did. The dominant stood immediately in front of him.

Keeping his gaze fixed on a point somewhere around the older man's knees, Devon tried not to look as fragile as he felt. He didn't glance up until Mr. Templeton tucked a knuckle under his chin and tilted his head back.

The older man rarely appeared impressed, but Devon realised in that moment that he'd never seen him so coldly furious before.

The clock began to strike. Mr. Templeton stared down at him in silence.

For several, long, terrifying seconds, Devon thought he wasn't going to say the words—that he didn't want to be his master any more, not even for one sodding hour.

"At the stroke of twelve on this day and on every weekday from now on, you will belong to me for one hour. Understand?"

Devon closed his eyes, relief flooding through him. "Thank you, sir."

"I asked you if you understand." His tone wasn't just cold, it was frigid.

Opening his eyes, Devon looked anxiously up at his master. "Yes, sir."

Mr. Templeton took a step back, putting enough distance between them that he could look him over properly. Devon had thought he was getting used to that, but this wasn't the cool, clinical look, or even the pleased, admiring one he was starting to see a little more often from his master. The dominant's anger hadn't disappeared when the hour started.

Mr. Templeton turned away from him and strode to the office door. "Follow me."

Devon trailed after him, his nerves increasing with every step. Mr. Templeton strode along the corridor leading towards the back of the building at such a pace, Devon had to scurry along to keep up with him.

At the end of the corridor was what looked like some kind of staff room where the people who worked in the building could take their breaks. Another door on the opposite side of the room led to a bathroom.

"Strip."

Devon breathed a sigh of relief. Everything was fine. Only the location had changed.

As Mr. Templeton turned on the taps above the bath and hot steam filled the room, Devon took his clothes off as quickly as his shivering would allow. With shaking hands, he folded them as tidily as he could and placed them on the vanity next to the sink.

"Get in."

Devon looked at the bath. An order was an order. Just because it was a new one, that didn't mean he shouldn't obey it. Some tiny part of his brain that the vodka hadn't killed off the night before remembered that Mr. Templeton was always pleased with him when he did as he was told. He lifted a foot and stepped over the high side of the tub.

The younger man almost toppled over as he snatched his foot away from the water. His hands caught hold of the edge of the bath just in time to keep him on his feet.

Looking over his shoulder, he found his master right behind him. "It's too hot, sir."

"Get in."

Devon looked back to the bath full of water. "Sir—"

"The water's fine. It only feels too hot because you're half frozen. Get in."

Devon looked from him to the water and back again. He put his foot back into the tub. Every inch of his skin that touched the liquid screamed out that it was scalding him. Somehow he still managed to lower his foot to the bottom of the tub. Gripping the sides so tightly his fingertips turned as white as the enamel on the tub, he forced himself to bring his other foot into the water too.

Closing his eyes for a moment, he desperately tried to push the throbbing heat away. His master might be angry as hell, but he wouldn't order him to scald himself from tip to toe. Even knowing that, Devon had to bite his lip to stop himself crying out as he slowly lowered himself into the steaming water.

It felt like someone had poured liquid fire into the bath. With each inch he descended, the water ignited yet more of his skin. Forcing his eyes open, he looked up at Mr. Templeton through the steam that swirled around the room. His master didn't look in the least sympathetic.

Devon dropped his gaze. Against all his expectations, his skin wasn't blistering under the onslaught of the water. As he sat in the bath, the pain slowly ebbed away and turned to pleasure. Heat seeped into his body, warming his chilled frame. He sighed his relief as he leant back in the blissful comfort of it.

"Did you actually make it to your bed at any point last night?" Mr. Templeton asked.

"It was Mike—one of my friend's—birthday, we went out and—" Devon caught his master's eye. The dominant didn't want details, just an answer to the question he had asked. "No, sir, I didn't."

"Anyone else's bed?"

Devon shook his head very rapidly. His brain spun. He covered his mouth, fighting against his queasiness. "I wouldn't do that, sir." He hadn't so much as looked at another man since he'd started visiting his master. He made an effort to pry his eyes open and met Mr. Templeton's gaze. It was important that his master believe that, but Devon couldn't tell if he did or not.

He dropped his gaze as Mr. Templeton continued to study him.

"I'm sorry, sir," he offered.

The dominant made no response.

After a while, Mr. Templeton ordered him to get washed. Through the whole process, he stayed by the side of the bath, watching him until he was finished.

"Get out."

He handed Devon a big white towel to dry himself off. While he rubbed the soft towelling against his skin and the water drained out of the bath, he saw his master leave the room. He came back as Devon began to cautiously rub the towel against his sore head.

He'd thought he was used to hangovers, but this one really was something special. Glancing at Mr. Templeton from beneath the edge of the towel, he tried to gauge his mood. He was just in time to see the older man place a small pile of clothes on the vanity next to the clothes

Devon had removed before his bath. A carrier bag was placed by the worn clothes.

"Come here."

Devon walked across the room to him. In spite of the soothing warmth of the bath he still ached all over. Every movement was an effort.

Lifting a hand, Mr. Templeton took hold of his chin and roughly turned Devon's head to one side then the other. Taking the towel from Devon, the older man rubbed at the especially sore point the younger man had been avoiding drying on his right temple.

A spike of discomfort flashed through him before the dominant finally took the towel away from his head. There was blood on it. Devon stared wide-eyed at the stained fabric. "Sir?"

Mr. Templeton glared down at him. "Do you remember what happened?"

Devon shook his head. "I must have fallen...?" he hazarded.

He tried to reach up and touch his temple as if that might help him remember, but his master caught hold of his chin once more and turned his head to the side.

Devon took the hint. He didn't have permission to do that. He dropped his hand back down to his side. After a few moments, Mr. Templeton seemed to lose interest in the cut. He caught hold of Devon's hand and lifted it to study his wrist. Following the dominant's gaze, Devon saw a red mark that promised to turn into a vivid bruise by the next day.

"And this?" Mr. Templeton asked.

"That was Jimmy," Devon said, pleased he could at least answer that question, if not any of the others the dominant might put to him. "I think he's one of my..." One night stands sounded wrong. "Exes?"

"You think?" the older man demanded.

Devon looked down. "I tend to get a bit fuzzy after a certain number of drinks, sir."

Mr. Templeton made him look back up. "If someone hurt you last night, you need to tell me." For the first time that day, there was a touch of something other than cold fury in his voice. There was something in his tone which said Devon could speak up, without fear, if there was something he *needed* to tell his master rather than if there was just something he wanted to babble about.

One brain cell nudged its neighbour. Devon realised what his master was asking him. "No, sir! He was just being an idiot. He wasn't trying to force me to do anything."

The older man studied Devon's eyes very seriously for several seconds, obviously judging his sincerity.

He nodded, just once, to indicate that he was willing to accept the answer. "Return to the office when you're dressed."

"Yes, sir." The words sounded lost and sad in the empty room. Mr. Templeton hadn't waited around to hear his answer.

For several long seconds, Devon stared at the door, but even hungover as hell, he was able to realise he wouldn't get back into the older man's good graces by being slow to obey his orders.

He turned to the clothes on the vanity. Examination of them proved that they were all exactly the right size for him. There was no way in hell they'd ever fitted his master.

Devon put the clothes on, smoothing them all neatly into place before he packed the rest of his clothes into the carrier bag and retraced the path to the office.

Mr. Templeton sat behind his desk, his expression more serious than ever. Devon stepped forward until he stood before it, the same way he had so many times before.

"Sit by the table," Mr. Templeton ordered. "Drink the coffee. Eat the soup."

Glancing behind him, Devon traced the fantastic scent of hot, rich food to a bowl of thick, creamy soup and a cup of coffee set on the small table on the other side of the room. His stomach rumbled, reminding him he hadn't eaten since early the previous afternoon. The food called to him, promising to ease his hangover and make him feel just a little bit better about the world.

"Thank you, sir."

Mr. Templeton didn't look up from his paperwork.

There was nothing else for Devon to do then but follow his master's orders. The soup and the coffee calmed his anxieties as they eased his hunger. His master couldn't be that pissed off with him if he was still willing to feed him. As soon as he'd finished both the coffee and the soup, the younger man looked across to Mr. Templeton for the next command.

His master didn't so much as glance in his direction.

Devon sat in silence.

A few seconds passed. He adjusted the hem on the thick woollen sweater his master had given him. Perhaps his master hadn't bought the clothes for him, perhaps they'd belonged to someone else once. But the fact Mr. Templeton had given them to him still meant something — it meant the dominant must still care about him, if only a little.

Minutes ticked past, and Devon found it harder and harder to sit in silence. "Is there anything I can do to help, sir?" he asked, when the quiet finally became too much for him.

Mr. Templeton didn't look up, or in any way acknowledge that Devon had spoken.

Suddenly it was obvious that neither the food nor the clothes meant a damn thing. Devon closed his eyes. His hands clenched around the edge of his sweater as he tried to push away just how much it hurt to have his master mad at him.

He failed completely. His efforts only made him hate himself more. It was stupid to have gone out and got so drunk like that. He knew he needed to be there for Mr. Templeton. Telling himself that everything would be fine so long as he made it there on time had been senseless too. His master deserved more than someone who was merely punctual.

More of their hour ticked past. Devon looked at the empty bowl and mug. If there was somewhere to heat the soup and make the coffee, there had to be somewhere he could wash up—maybe in the bathroom he'd just visited.

He glanced across at his master, but he couldn't even bring himself to speak up and ask for permission to do that. He wrapped his arms around his torso as the frigid atmosphere seemed to seep into his bones and steal all the warmth he'd found in his master's provisions for him that day.

By the time the clock began to strike one, his view of the desk top was blurring. Devon brushed at his eyes with the back of his hand, determined not to make things worse by making his master think he was going for the sympathy vote.

The clock fell silent.

"You may leave."

Devon stood up, very slowly. He looked at the door, but his feet carried him to his spot on the rug.

"Sir?" The word sounded weak and lost, but that didn't matter right then. He had to ask. He had to know.

Mr. Templeton looked up.

Devon had to clear his throat before he could make more words happen. "Am I still allowed to come back tomorrow, sir?"

"Twelve until one," Mr. Templeton said.

Devon closed his eyes. For the first time since he'd begun to doubt he'd be welcomed the next day, he felt like he could breathe without something stabbing him in the chest. "Thank you, sir."

Mr. Templeton turned back to his work without a word.

Several minutes passed in silence as Templeton stared blindly down at the paperwork before him. He closed his eyes for a moment.

The boy was fine. No real harm had been done. Knowing that didn't make it any easier for him to push aside the pure terror that had raced through him when he saw the blood on his temple and the bruise on his wrist.

Yes, he had potential. There couldn't be any doubt about that. Devon was as instinctive a submissive as any man could be—and far more in need of a master's guidance than any boy Templeton had ever laid eyes on.

Rising from his chair, the dominant crossed the room and picked up the mug and bowl from the table.

Natural submission only counted for so much. An hour a day could only make a certain amount of impact on a man's path through life. Templeton nodded slowly to himself as he reached his decision.

It was time to take another step forwards.

Chapter Three

Friday 12th February 2010

Devon was waiting patiently for his master to unlock the door for him at five minutes to the hour. As soon as he heard the lock turn over, he carefully pushed the door open. Mr. Templeton was just stepping back into his office. He didn't turn and look over his shoulder as Devon trailed after him.

The clothes the dominant had given him the day before were in a carrier bag. They bounced against Devon's leg as he quickly made his way to his place in front of the desk.

Falling still, Devon silently waited for Mr. Templeton to speak with the chimes of the clock.

"At the stroke of twelve on this day and on every weekday from now on, you will belong to me for one hour. Do you understand?"

"Yes, sir. Thank you, sir."

Mr. Templeton's attention dropped to the carrier bag in Devon's hand.

"I wasn't sure if…" he held out the bag of neatly folded and laundered clothes towards the older man.

Mr. Templeton shook his head. "Keep them."

"Thank you, sir." Devon lowered his arm back to his side, hoping that was a positive sign.

"Put them, and the clothes you're wearing, on the desk."

"Yes, sir."

Devon quickly and efficiently removed his clothes, folded them with practiced ease and placed them on the table, next to the carrier bag. The familiarity of the actions soothed him. His master allowed him to do as he had always done. It was a very good sign.

Rising from the chair behind his desk, Mr. Templeton crossed the room to sit on the sofa set in the far corner. As Devon watched, the older man picked up a cushion and placed it on the floor at his feet. "Come here, Devon."

He hurried across and lowered himself to his knees before his master, unable to work out if he should be excited or nervous about this new development.

The only thing he could be sure of was that it was *very something*. He just didn't know if it was going to be very good or very bad.

"You're aware that we need to discuss your behaviour yesterday."

"Yes, sir." Devon looked up and met the dominant's eyes. In a strange way, it was a relief to have the topic out in the open. Even as he squirmed slightly on the cushion, he listened eagerly to hear what the other man had to say.

"Arriving here in that condition is entirely unacceptable," Mr. Templeton told him.

Devon nodded. "Yes, sir."

"Do you have anything you wish to say about it?"

"I really didn't mean things to turn out that way, sir," Devon blurted out, before he could think better of it. "I was only going to have one or two drinks, then..."

"Then?" the dominant prompted.

Devon looked down. "I did switch to soft drinks for a while, but everyone else was still knocking back vodka and..."

"And your friends thought your behaviour was amusing," Mr. Templeton filled in for him.

Devon nodded, still staring down at his master's feet.

Mr. Templeton made him look up. "And what do *you* think of the way you behaved?"

"I screwed up, sir," Devon said.

"Yes."

He blinked up at his master.

For a moment, Mr. Templeton looked almost amused. "Did you think I'd lie and tell you that I don't care if you go out and get so drunk you can't find your way home, keep yourself safe or conduct yourself with any sort of dignity?"

"I—" Devon cut himself off before he could make things even worse than they already were.

"You?" Mr. Templeton prompted.

Devon shook his head and looked away. "I'm sorry, sir."

"Finish the sentence," he ordered, making Devon meet his eyes once more.

"I turned up on time, sir," Devon whispered.

"Yes. And I can tell that you went to a great deal of effort to make sure you did — which is good. But, I expect more than that from you now. The way you behave during the other twenty-three hours in a day alters the way you're able to conduct yourself during the hour you belong to me."

"Yes, sir."

"And this is the worst part of it all." Reaching out, Mr. Templeton gently caressed Devon's injured temple. He studied the damaged skin for several moments before holding out his hand.

Devon offered up his injured wrist to be inspected, too. When he seemed satisfied that his injuries weren't serious, his master released Devon's hand.

"If you are to belong to me, even for an hour a day, you'll have to learn to take better care of yourself."

If...Devon swallowed rapidly. "It won't happen again, sir," he promised.

Mr. Templeton stared down at him for several minutes, as if debating with himself what he should say next.

Devon held his breath until the older man finally made his decision. "Your behaviour yesterday was a symptom, not the whole problem, Devon. What do you do during the hours you don't spend with me?"

Devon shrugged. "Not much, sir."

"And do you think that's adequate?"

"I don't really need to do anything, sir. My grandfather left me quite a bit of money when he passed away and..." He trailed off when he caught sight of his master's expression.

"That merely means you don't need the money you could earn from a job," the older man corrected. "Not that you don't need employment."

"You want me to get a job?" Devon guessed.

"I want you to think of a better use of your time than going out and getting drunk, or idling your days away doing *not much* with your life."

"I could come here —"

Mr. Templeton's fingertips silenced him. "No, something else." He took his fingers away.

Devon frowned down at his own hands. "I'm not sure there's anything I'm much use for," he admitted softly. "I didn't really get on well with school, and even when I did get a job I..." He trailed off, wondering, not for the first time, why Mr. Templeton would want him of all people hanging around him, even for an hour.

"Don't you think those are things you should start to correct?" his master asked.

Devon nodded. "Yes, sir."

Mr. Templeton stroked his fingers through Devon's hair, just once. "It's something I want you to start thinking about very seriously."

"Yes, sir," he said again.

Mr. Templeton nodded. It looked almost like approval, except it couldn't possibly be that. Devon knelt quietly at his feet for a few minutes, wondering if that was it and half hoping it wasn't.

"What are you thinking?" Mr. Templeton asked him after a few moments.

"You didn't punish me yesterday, sir," Devon pointed out tentatively.

"No, I didn't."

"I thought you would," Devon whispered.

"You were in no condition to be punished yesterday. And a punishment should never be delivered in anger."

"What about today, sir?" Devon blurted out.

"Are you telling me you want to be punished?"

"Yes, sir." He hadn't even realised just how much he wanted it until the words passed his lips.

No, wanted was the wrong word, it felt far more like something he needed—an aching desperation for it settled in the base of his soul as he came face to face with the possibility for the first time.

Mr. Templeton made him look up and meet his gaze once more. "Think very carefully before you ask me for any sort of punishment, Devon. If you want me to provide you with closure after your mistakes I will. You'll be punished and the matter we're dealing with won't be spoken of or thought of again afterwards. But the punishment will always be a real punishment, not a game, and it'll hurt."

Devon forced himself to hold the other man's gaze through every word. "I understand, sir. I am asking to be punished."

Mr. Templeton nodded, just once. "Stand up."

Swallowing down his nerves, Devon did as he was commanded.

"Over my lap."

After all the things Devon had imagined the punishment might include, a spanking didn't seem that bad. He was reasonably sure could get through a spanking without letting his master down. That thought alone sent a wave of relief rushing through him.

Taking half a step forward, he looked at his master's lap and found he didn't have the least idea how the hell he was supposed to turn himself over it. The older man offered him no encouragement, no advice. Devon was left to clumsily scramble into place as best he could.

He almost toppled onto the floor, before his master's arm finally settled over the small of his back and held him exactly where Mr. Templeton wanted him to be.

Taking a deep breath, Devon braced himself for the first stroke, but several seconds passed, and it didn't come.

"This is about learning self control as much as it's about punishment," the dominant informed him. "If you ask me to stop, I'll end the punishment immediately, and you won't be allowed to change your mind. Understand?"

"Yes, sir," Devon whispered. He squirmed, unable to hold himself still as his nerves built up.

The first strike landed heavily and without warning on his upturned arse. Devon flinched, gasping at the force of it. He thought he'd been spanked in the past. A few guys had wanted to mess about before, but with the first connection of Mr. Templeton's hand on his backside Devon realised this was in a different league.

This wasn't a tap to make his buttocks blush before someone screwed him. It was a punishment, and Mr. Templeton had warned him from the start that punishments were supposed to hurt.

The older man's hand came down on the other cheek. Devon closed his eyes, biting down on his bottom lip to keep from making any sound. He mentally counted out the first dozen spanks. Then, numbers failed him. All he could do after that was repeat over and over inside his head that he couldn't let a single word pass his lips.

He couldn't let Mr. Templeton down by asking him to stop before his master was ready to declare the punishment over.

Tears flooded his eyes. Devon squeezed his lids shut very tight, begging the tears not to fall. They fell anyway, and there was nothing he could do about it. The heat and pain flaring across his arse paled in comparison to how much it hurt to let his master down that way.

He bit his lip until he tasted blood, desperately trying not to cry out as the sound of hand against skin filled the air again and again, and each time a wave of heat and pain flared under Devon's skin in response. The spanks came in quick succession, allowing him no time to recover from the last, and each one was delivered with the same harsh force.

His master held nothing back. Devon's arse burned, his skin screamed in protest as a blaze seared through the nerve endings. Every muscle in Devon's body tensed. His hands curled into fists. His legs twitched as he fought against the urge to kick out.

Then, silence.

Devon lay across his master's lap, his breaths coming in pants and his eyes shut so tightly fireworks exploded behind the lids, waiting for whatever would come next.

"Turn over, Devon."

More clumsy than ever, trembling as he tried to coordinate his movements, Devon scrambled to do as his master commanded. On his third attempt, he managed to turn himself the right way up.

Mr. Templeton guided him to sit on his lap. A new wave of agony flooded him as his weight came to rest on his buttocks. Devon bit back a yelp. He turned his face away, as if there was any chance his master wouldn't see his tears.

It didn't do him any good. The older man made him turn back and look him in the eye.

Devon swiped at the tear tracks with the back of his hand.

"I'm so sorry, sir." The words were barely a whisper.

Deftly brushing his hand aside, Mr. Templeton wiped the tears away himself. One of his hands was pleasantly warm as he held Devon's head still to swipe the moisture away with his thumb. The other palm was burning hot.

Its touch shocked Devon into realising that he wasn't the only one his punishment had hurt. He quickly caught his master's hand and kissed the palm, trying to soothe the other man's pain.

Mr. Templeton allowed it for a few seconds, before calmly taking his hand out of Devon's hold. Guiding

Devon to lean into his body, Mr. Templeton encouraged him to rest his head on his shoulder. He stroked his fingers through Devon's hair and just let him rest in his embrace for a little while.

"Hush. You're fine now."

Devon swallowed rapidly. He nodded into his master's shoulder as his breaths slowly steadied. As hard as he tried not to squirm, it was impossible for him to sit still right then. He'd never imagined a spanking could hurt so much.

As he wriggled, trying and failing to find a less painful way to sit, he slowly became aware that his squirming was getting his master hard. He glanced up at the older man, doubtful he'd be granted the privilege of servicing him after the way he had behaved.

"I really am sorry, sir," he whispered again.

Mr. Templeton stroked his fingers down Devon's cheek. "You took the punishment very well. The matter is forgotten."

Devon hesitated. "Really, sir?"

"I wouldn't say so otherwise, would I?"The dominant's voice was surprisingly gentle.

"No, sir," Devon said.

His master wouldn't humour him with lies. He knew that. Devon met his gaze, still not sure how to offer himself to the other man. Mr. Templeton smiled a fraction and tapped the cushion that rested on the floor with his foot.

No further order was required. Devon quickly slid off his lap to kneel at his feet. A nod was all the permission he needed. His hands still shaking, his mind swirling with the pain flaring outwards from his buttocks, Devon freed Mr. Templeton's erection from his clothes as quickly as he could and took him eagerly into his mouth.

He'd paid attention to every instruction his master had given him over his previous attempts to please him. He sucked gently and steadily around the tip of his shaft, lavishing his tongue's attention on the head. Lapping and swirling around the glans, he worked the older man exactly the way he'd learnt Mr. Templeton liked best.

A few moments passed, and his master stroked his hair back, the way he only ever did when Devon had pleased him in some way. No orders, no corrections, Mr. Templeton didn't find one single fault with him as he knelt at his feet and savoured every taste he could glean from his master.

Even when he eventually allowed the dominant's softening cock to slip from his lips at the older man's command, Devon found that he wasn't pushed away. He was still allowed to rest his head against the dominant's thigh and have his hair stroked and petted.

Mr. Templeton permitted him to remain exactly where he was until the clock struck one. Hiding his face in the older man's lap, Devon only looked up at his master when Mr. Templeton touched his cheek to get his attention.

"Put your clothes back on, Devon."

Devon reluctantly did as he was ordered. His backside was still an inferno. Every movement only increased the ache in the muscles. It took every scrap of self control Devon could muster not to reach behind him and rub at the flaming skin, to try and ease the sting.

Putting his trousers on was a lesson in just how rough denim could be. Devon tried not to let the discomfort show on his face. He'd asked for the punishment. It was worth a little soreness to be rid of the guilt he'd felt for letting his master down.

As soon as he was dressed, he walked across to the door, but he couldn't help but look back at his master one last time.

"Tomorrow," Mr. Templeton said with a nod, as he returned to his desk.

Devon nodded. "Thank you, sir."

The door closed softly behind Devon. Templeton leant back in his chair and took a deep breath as he continued to stare at the woodwork long after the boy had left the building. When he finally looked away, his gaze fell on his right hand. His left thumb was massaging the palm, absentmindedly trying to ease the ache in it.

Letting out a sigh, Templeton tried to turn back to his work. It had been the right thing to do. It had been exactly what Devon had needed in order to draw a line under the whole mess.

Still, part of him couldn't quite help but regret that the boy's first introduction to being spanked had been about pain rather than pleasure.

Soon, he promised himself. As soon as Devon was ready for it...

Chapter Four

Thursday 18th March 2010

"At the stroke of twelve on this day and every day from now on, you will belong to me for one hour. Do you understand?"

"Every day?" Devon snatched at the word. "Really?"

Mr. Templeton raised an eyebrow, although there was amusement in his eyes as well as a note of correction.

Devon cleared his throat. "Yes, sir," he said, as seriously as he could manage, even though he couldn't quite wipe the smile off his face.

Mr. Templeton ruffled his hair with casual affection as he walked past him to stand on the other side of the room. "Undress, then come here, Devon."

He immediately stripped off and went to his master's side. The dominant stood by the small desk with the green leather inlay. Devon was pretty sure he was well on the way to developing one hell of a fetish for that table—

especially since visiting it usually meant he had a chance to come.

As much as he loved dropping to his knees and sucking his master's cock, he'd left the office hard and frustrated for eleven visits in a row. Including the weekends, when he hadn't been permitted to visit until now, he hadn't been allowed to come for sixteen, very, *very* long days.

"Sit on the desk."

Devon did as he was told without even thinking to question the order. He lifted his backside up on the desk and eagerly cooperated as Mr. Templeton began to arrange him just as he wanted him, lying back across the leather, his knees spread and pulled back to his chest, and his arse resting right on the edge of the table.

The dominant looked him over for a few minutes, as if debating whether or not he should be rearranged. Finally he nodded. He didn't hesitate for a single moment once his decision had been made. Slicked fingers soon slid into Devon's exposed hole and began to stretch him gradually open.

Already way past the point where he thought anything he did would change his master's chosen pace, all Devon could do was close his eyes and enjoy every moment. Holding his legs back the way his master wanted, he just relished every touch of his master's fingers and gloried in the other man's attention.

When the dominant's hands eventually disappeared and clothes rustled, Devon blinked his eyes open. He was just in time to watch his master sheath himself in a condom and spread a little extra lube over the latex.

The first thrust, as his master buried himself deep inside him, made Devon gasp. Still holding back his legs, he dug his fingers into his calves.

He wanted to come. He needed to come. Desperation raced through him. But it would still be incredibly embarrassing if he didn't manage to last for the first thirty seconds. Anyone who was worthy of belonging to Mr. Templeton should be able to last longer than that.

Devon closed his eyes and frantically tried to hold on to his control for just a little longer.

"Open your eyes, Devon. Look at me."

He tried to obey, to focus on his master through clouds of arousal. Their eyes met.

"You don't have permission to come. Understand?"

Devon opened his lips to protest. The chances of his control actually holding out were so unlikely, Devon didn't even know how to begin to explain the situation to his master.

"Yes, sir." The words left his mouth, but they were only really an acknowledgement that he'd heard what his master had said and understood the words. He didn't think for a moment that he'd actually be able to follow the order.

Mr. Templeton's hips rocked forward, burying his cock to the hilt in the younger man's arse once more, every inch of his length making Devon more convinced than ever that he'd never outlast his master.

Devon whimpered as thrust after thrust pounded into his prostate. Pre-cum leaked from the tip of his cock and dripped onto his stomach. He held back with every ounce of his strength. Then, just when he knew it was a lost cause and there was no way he could continue to follow the other man's order, he felt Mr. Templeton's rhythm falter.

The older man's grip around his hips tightened for a moment. Pleasure flashed across his face as he came deep inside Devon with a last few hard thrusts, before stilling inside him, looking straight down into his eyes.

Devon stared helplessly back at him, unable to break the gaze. When his master pulled away to tidy himself up, Devon closed his eyes and repeated over and over inside his head that his coming wasn't that important, even if it did feel as important as hell in that moment.

He was with his master, and his master was pleased with him. Nothing else was as vital as that. Nothing else was significant at all.

"Your self control is coming along very well, Devon," Mr. Templeton said, as he moved back to stand at the edge of the desk between his legs.

"Thank you, sir," Devon whispered, his voice rough with arousal and emotion.

The older man stood there looking down at him for quite some time before he, quite casually, bent down and took his submissive's cock between his lips. Devon helplessly bucked into the lush, warm wetness.

"Sir?" he managed, through gritted teeth.

Mr. Templeton pulled back. Devon's cock slipped from his mouth. He looked down at him. "Yes?"

"My self control isn't *that* good, sir," he blurted out.

His master's lips twitched into another of those rare half-smiles. "Then it's a good thing you now have my permission to come." He lowered his head again then, as if that explained everything, as if him going down on Devon was the most natural thing in the world.

Devon looked down his body and watched as Mr. Templeton slowly parted his lips and took his whole shaft into his mouth. Cradling Devon's balls in his hand, he rolled the tight sac between his fingers as he suckled rhythmically around the glans.

Staring down at the older man Devon desperately tried to wrap his head around the fact that his master wasn't only willing to give his submissive head, but that he was bloody fantastic at it. It wasn't easy, especially not when his entire brain seemed to melt further by the moment. His head swirled with pleasure. His fingertips bit into the backs of his legs as he scrambled for control.

But still, no matter how much he tried to make it last, it wasn't possible to remain in the perfect cocoon of his master's mouth for more than a few minutes. Devon's hips rocked up off the table. He came before he could think to issue a warning. Staring down his body, he could only watch fascinated as Mr. Templeton calmly swallowed it all down without missing a single damn drop.

Slack jawed, he gawped incredulously at his master as the older man straightened up. Mr. Templeton chuckled and stroked Devon's cheek with his knuckle before he walked back to his desk and calmly sat down. "When you're ready, come across and sit with me."

Devon took that to mean he had a few minutes to get his breath back and be sure his legs would support him before he walked across the room. He needed those minutes. His body didn't seem to be his to control anymore. Even when his breaths evened out and his heart ceased to race so fast, it was hard for him to pull himself together and rise from the desk.

It wasn't so much readiness as the need to kneel by his master's chair and rest his head on his knee that finally brought him across the room.

They sat in silence for several minutes. Finally Devon built up the courage to speak.

"Sir?"

"Yes, Devon?" His tone invited further speech.

"What you said before," Devon began. "About how you think it would be a good idea if I got a job…"

"Yes?"

"I was jogging in the park opposite my flat a few days ago and I got talking to an old friend," he thought about that sentence for a second and decided it sounded wrong, as if he was meeting up with men who weren't his master in the park. "He's straight and married and everything."

Mr. Templeton calmly nodded for him to continue.

"He works with this charity—a wildlife trust—and he said they were looking for volunteers. And he asked if I'd be interested in working with them some mornings."

Devon stared down at where his hand rested on his own knee. "I wouldn't be doing anything special, just helping out. I spoke to him again yesterday. I told him I wouldn't be able to work after eleven. He said that would be okay. So, I'd still be able to come here every day and…" He glanced up at his master, wondering if the babbled explanation made any sense let alone found favour with him.

"You don't need my permission to do whatever you want during the hours you don't spend with me, Devon," Mr. Templeton told him. "But, if you want my opinion, I think that sounds like a very good idea." He stroked his hair and smiled down at him.

Devon nodded his understanding. Whatever the older man said, he saw the truth in the dominant's eyes. He had his master's approval. That was all he needed to know.

* * * *

Tuesday 13th April 2010

The door was already unlocked when Devon arrived at seven minutes to twelve. He frowned and cautiously stepped inside, wondering if one of the secretaries Mr. Templeton liked to send on long lunch breaks had yet to leave.

Someone was speaking French in Mr. Templeton's office — someone with a very familiar voice that called to Devon, even while it was speaking a different language. Devon peeped around the half open door. His master sat alone in the room, speaking into the phone. Walking across to the spot on the rug where he always waited, the submissive looked to his master for further instruction.

Mr. Templeton rattled off a few quick words of French before putting the phone to one side and pressing a button on the hand set, which Devon took to mean the person he'd been speaking to was now on hold.

"I'm going to be on the phone for most of the hour."

Panic rushed through Devon the moment the words hit the air. Mr. Templeton couldn't send him away, just like that. He had to have his hour with his master.

"Please, may I stay anyway, sir? I swear, you won't hear a word from me. I'll just sit quietly and stay out of your way."

He whispered the words very softly, as if that might somehow prove to his master just how quiet he could be. But Mr. Templeton just raised a hand for him to be completely silent. The older man pressed the button on the phone and spoke into the receiver once more.

A few minutes passed. The clock in the hall began to chime the hour, but Mr. Templeton was still deeply absorbed in his phone call. For several terrifying seconds Devon thought the dominant wasn't even going to have time to say the words to him. At the very last moment, he said a few quick words of French and pressed the hold button again.

He looked across at Devon and met his gaze. "At the stroke of twelve on this day and on every day from now on, you will belong to me for one hour. Understand?"

"Yes, sir." Relief made him sigh the words.

"Take your clothes off, then come here." Mr. Templeton tapped the floor by his feet with the toe of his shoe.

As the older man turned his attention back to his phone call, Devon did as he said and moved to sit, naked, by his master's feet.

It wasn't until that moment, when he sat practically ignored, that he realised how much just being owned by the other man for that one hour every day meant to him.

The sex was good. The sex was hot. Hell, it was bloody fantastic. But it was the pleasure of being owned that made him arrange his day around the hour he spent with his master. It was the other man's dominance that made him wonder what his master would think of whatever he was doing as he went through the other twenty-three hours of each day, not his cock.

It was pure mastery that was pushing him to work hard at the wildlife trust, and to drag himself to evening classes several times a week in the hopes of getting a few of those qualifications he hadn't been willing to work for in school.

Devon looked up and pushed his daydreams aside when Mr. Templeton touched his cheek. A crook of the older man's finger brought Devon to his feet. His master pressed another button on the phone, switching it to speaker phone.

Rapid French filled the air from the other end of the line.

Mr. Templeton put his finger against Devon's lips.

Devon nodded his understanding. Any noise he made would go straight to the man on the other side of the phone.

Taking Devon's hand in his, the dominant guided his submissive to wrap his hand around his half hard cock and begin to stroke himself with long, slow movements. A tap of his shoe on the floor boards and Devon lowered himself back to his knees, his hand still working his cock.

Every time he glanced up, Devon found his master watching him. While he rattled off French to the man on the other end of the line, while he listened to the swift response issued to whatever it was he'd said, no matter what he was doing, his eyes never left his submissive.

Devon's hand moved up and down his shaft again and again, first coaxing himself fully hard, then teasing himself to the edge.

With no sign that permission to come would be granted, Devon had no choice but to slow his touch and to stop himself just short of coming each time he approached the point of no return. It was obvious he couldn't climax until he received an order to do so, but at the same time, he knew couldn't stop jacking his cock either.

The minutes ticked by. His cock screamed in protest. The muscles in his hand and arm began to tire too. Devon started to listen out for the next set of chimes from the hallway. There was no way in hell he'd be able to last the whole hour of teasing himself like that.

Except he knew that if it was what his master wanted, he'd just have to bloody well find a way to do it, just as he'd had to find a way to ignore his friends' teasing when he stopped after two drinks, just as he'd found a way to build up the courage to book those courses at the local college.

His master always somehow made him capable of doing things he knew he was incapable of when the order was first issued.

Two piece of plastic clicked together as Mr. Templeton hung up the phone.

Devon didn't look up. He didn't stop jacking himself off, either. That wasn't his choice to make right then.

"That's enough."

Devon dropped his aching hand from his cock and dragged a deep, relieved breath into his body.

"Tell me about your class last night."

Devon cleared his throat and tried to remember that there was ever a time when he hadn't been sitting on the floor by his master's desk, stroking his cock and desperately trying not to come.

"We're studying *Great Expectations* this week. I got seventy-six percent on my last essay," he offered. He couldn't help but glance up at his master then, both eager and wary to see what his reaction might be.

Mr. Templeton nodded his approval. He half-smiled down at him. "Very good. That's the highest mark yet, isn't it?"

Devon nodded and smiled back. His master always asked. Every Tuesday since the course started, he'd asked how it was going, and listened to his little successes and failures, all with that same approving look in his eye.

His concerns obviously weren't as important as his master's. Devon knew that without either of them needing to acknowledge it aloud, but still...he always asked.

"Did your call go well?" Devon cautiously enquired in return, unsure if he was allowed to ask such questions of his master.

Mr. Templeton merely nodded. "Yes, it did."

Devon mentally added French to the end of the whole list of things he should try to learn at some point.

The moment was so companionable, so perfect, the clock chimes took him off guard.

A quick look at Mr. Templeton's crotch told Devon that he wasn't the only one left frustrated by the hour they'd spent together. "If you wanted me to stay a little longer," he offered, carefully.

Mr. Templeton didn't look angry with the suggestion. He even stroked Devon's cheek in approval for him making it, but he still shook his head.

"Twelve o'clock tomorrow," the older man said.

Devon pushed aside his disappointment. "Yes, sir."

* * * *

Saturday May 29th 2010

"At the stroke of twelve on this day and on every Saturday from now on, you will belong to me for twenty-four hours. Do you understand?"

Devon was so used to saying 'yes, sir', he almost didn't notice the slight but important change in what he was agreeing to. He opened his mouth.

Twenty-four hours.

His lips came back together without any actual words leaving them as the words registered.

"Is that a problem?" Mr. Templeton asked.

Devon shook his head. "No problem, sir. I understand. Thank you."

Even as his mind reeled, Devon struggled to pull the tattered edges of his composure together. He straightened his back and arranged himself a little more neatly in his place before the dominant's desk.

As he watched, the older man picked up his briefcase and walked towards the office door. Devon looked from him to the desk where he always left his clothes and back again. His hands had already gone automatically to the hem of his shirt. The change from their normal routine left him momentarily lost, without any point of reference to rely on. For several long seconds, all he could do was stand in the middle of the room and fidget with the edge of the fabric that had never lingered long on his skin while in that room.

"With me, Devon."

"Yes, sir." The order snapped him out of the deepest part of his daze. He dropped his hand to his side and trailed behind the other man as Mr. Templeton left the building and conscientiously locked the door behind them. When his master walked across to the only car parked in the driveway, Devon couldn't bring himself to step forward and approach the vehicle without a very clear invitation.

The moment seemed far too fragile, far too liable to end with him being dismissed in disgrace.

"You're to ride in the front passenger seat unless you're specifically told otherwise," Mr. Templeton informed him, as he unlocked the car.

"Yes, sir." The gravel crunched under Devon's own well polished shoes as he stepped forward and took his stated place in the other man's car.

Briefcase deposited in the boot, Mr. Templeton folded his larger frame into the car, next to Devon. His presence seemed to fill the entire space the moment he closed the driver's side door.

When Mr. Templeton fastened his seat belt, Devon quickly did the same. He rode in silence next to his master as Mr. Templeton drove them away from the office and into a different part of town.

Dividing his attention between the dominant and their surroundings, Devon frantically tried to work out what kind of mood the other man was in, and where they might be going. By the time the car pulled up outside a large Victorian house, he still had no idea of the other man's emotions, but a glance at the building hinted that they might have arrived at the most unexpected of locations.

"Is this your home, sir?"

"Yes."

Nothing else was said as Mr. Templeton led him inside.

Devon swallowed rapidly as he looked around the hallway. The house had the feel of a building that had been occupied by just one man for a long time, a man who was used to having things exactly as he liked them and who had expertly moulded the house to fit his personality and his preferences.

Everything was spotless. Without any sense of ostentation, every single object in the building seemed to exude quality. Devon looked at the well polished floor, then at his shoes, unsure if he should take them off. His fingers went to the edge of his shirt again, not sure if that should come off too or if being here was different to being in his master's office.

Mr. Templeton strode through a doorway leading off the hallway to the right. Devon crept forwards to peek inside. The older man stood by a table on the other side of a large living room. Mail had been placed on the table, along with a note, presumably from some sort of housekeeper.

"You may come in," Mr. Templeton said, without even looking over his shoulder.

Devon stepped forward until he stood in the centre of a rug in front of the fireplace, as he instinctively sought out the equivalent of his place in his master's office.

Someone had laid out logs in the hearth. It looked as if they only needed to have a match set to them to create a welcoming blaze. Devon wished like hell he had any confidence in his ability to tend a real fire without risking burning down his master's house. It might have made him feel just a little less useless.

A few seconds passed in silence. Mr. Templeton turned towards him. "Do you have a question, Devon?"

He cleared his throat. "May I know what the rules are here, sir?"

"Is there any reason you're so keen to know?" There was no bite to the question, just curiosity.

"I don't want to screw this up, sir." They might not have been the right words to say but Devon blurted them out anyway. They were the truth, and that was all he had to offer his master right then.

Mr. Templeton held his gaze in silence for several long seconds before crossing to sit on the sofa facing him. A nod to the floor by his feet had Devon kneeling on the rug directly before him.

"The rules are very simple. You still have the right to say no, and to leave whenever you wish. There's a phone in the hallway which you may use to call a taxi and enough money in the drawer below the phone to pay the fare."

Devon shook his head.

"I'm not accusing you of asking to leave," Mr. Templeton cut in before Devon had a chance to say a single word. "I'm giving you information. You may ask any questions when I'm finished."

"Yes, sir," Devon whispered.

"While you're here, I expect you to obey whatever orders I give you, and complete any tasks you're assigned, just as you would at my office. If you have any immediate questions or concerns you may raise them. And if there are any more general issues that you wish to discuss with me, there will be time for you to broach those topics too."

He stopped, as if waiting for an answer. "Yes, sir." It was the obvious thing to say.

"When you don't have a task to occupy you, then you may relax. On the other side of the entrance hall, there's a library and you have free use of the books in there."

"Thank you, sir."

"You may pick out something to read this evening while I get changed."

Mr. Templeton stood up. Devon strode after him as he left the room. It took all the self control he could scrape together to change course in the hall and make his way to the opposite doorway rather than stalk the other man up the stairs.

A library. It was a perfectly accurate description of the room, but the reality of it still made him stop in his tracks. Devon had never seen so many books owned by one man before. As he silently ran his gaze along row upon row of leather bound spines, he felt himself falling further and further out of his depth by the moment.

Finally his attention settled on a shelf containing obviously newer books. He stepped forwards until he stood directly in front of it, hoping like hell he'd at least find a title he recognised, or a subject he had some chance of understanding.

A frown grew across Devon's forehead as he found not one familiar title, but an entire shelf full of them.

It was like scanning through his entire reading list for every course he was taking or was due to start within the next three months. Reaching out, he ran his fingers down the spines. There wasn't a single crease where any of them had been opened. None of them had been read. They obviously weren't books Mr. Templeton had simply had laying around.

"Devon?"

He jumped as he spun around to face the older man. He blinked at his master as if he'd never seen him before. In a way, he never had seen him as he appeared right then, in jeans and a comfortable sweater rather than one of his expensive suits.

Mr. Templeton raised an eyebrow at him. "Is there a problem?"

"No, sir." You're gorgeous! He kept the last words back somehow.

The older man took a step back, towards the door. "Leave your choice in the living room on the way past."

"Yes, sir." Devon quickly found the next book he needed to read for his English Literature course and followed the dominant from the room. A few minutes later, when he found himself standing in Mr. Templeton's kitchen, he wished he'd chosen to take a cookery course instead.

Suddenly, his ability to heat up a microwave meal didn't count for much.

"Sir?"

"Yes, Devon?"

"I can't cook," he blurted out, eager to get the admission over with as soon as possible. "I mean—"

"Then it's time you started to learn," Mr. Templeton cut in briskly, as he pushed his sleeves halfway up his forearms. "You can start by fetching four eggs for me." He pointed to a container on the counter top.

"You can cook," Devon realised.

Mr. Templeton's lips twitched, almost as if he was about to smile. "Yes," he agreed, his tone still perfectly solemn. "I can."

The words sunk into Devon's mind as easily as every other pronouncement the older man had ever made, but there was still some little part of him that just stared at the sight of his master in his kitchen as if he'd been beamed down from another planet.

Apparently, the planet his master came from bred dominants who didn't think cooking was strictly submissives' work. Mr. Templeton moved around the large, light space as if he didn't just own it, but as if he commanded it too. Complete confidence, complete control of the whole world.

It was almost like helping him out in the office—the older man soon found lots of little jobs for him to do. Almost like helping him in his office, except as Devon watched him work, his gaze strayed to the muscles in his forearms. He'd never even seen that much of him bare before.

It was all he could do to keep his hands by his sides and not reach out to stroke the older man's skin.

"Are you listening, Devon?"

He snapped his attention up to his master's eyes. A lie rushed to his lips, but he bit it back. "No, sir. I was daydreaming," he confessed.

Mr. Templeton held his gaze for a moment. He didn't look half so furious as Devon would have imagined he'd be. That tiny touch of a smile came back. If nothing else, he seemed to appreciate his submissive's honesty. His tone of voice was warm when he spoke. "There'll be time for daydreaming later. Right now, I want you to concentrate."

"Yes, sir." Devon did his best, but simply being with the Mr. Templeton in his house was distracting. As they sat down to eat the meal the dominant had prepared for them, Devon couldn't help but want to spend all his time staring at him and simply soaking up his presence, but somehow the food still made it to his lips as a companionable silence settled over them.

"Tell me about your family," Mr. Templeton suddenly ordered, as they finished off the last of the meal.

Devon blinked at him. "Sir?"

"Your family," Mr. Templeton repeated. "Tell me about them."

Their plates were empty. Devon shrugged as he picked up his fork and traced the sparse pattern on the chinaware. "There's not much to tell, sir."

"Your parents are still alive?"

"Last I heard they were," Devon said, more softly than he'd intended. He cleared his throat and pushed on. His master appreciated him telling the truth, and it was his master who was important now, not them. "We haven't spoken much since I came out. That was kind of the final straw for them."

He glanced up to check the other man's reaction.

"The other straws being?" Mr. Templeton asked, his expression entirely neutral.

Devon set down his fork and pushed his plate away. "Lack of intelligence. Lack of talent. Lack of finesse. Lack of ambition. Lack of charm. Lack of whatever it was they were looking for in a son." He stared at the table directly in front of him as the pain from every word they'd ever thrown at him flooded back into his body.

Part of him was suddenly so sure that the older man was going to realise that they were right—and that he'd been right to waste his time doing nothing much at all, because that was all he was really capable of.

Mr. Templeton stood up. Devon closed his eyes for a moment, but he couldn't bring himself to beg—that wouldn't be fair on his master. "I'll just get my coat, sir."

"Devon?"

Pushing his own chair back, Devon turned towards the door. "I won't bother you again, sir."

Suddenly a hand was wrapped around his wrist, tight and perfect. Devon automatically tried to pull away, but the fingers tightened against his skin. He wasn't going anywhere.

He looked up and met the older man's eyes for a moment.

"Do you really think I'd bring you here if I agreed with anything you just said to me—anything that they said to you?" Mr. Templeton demanded.

Devon swallowed.

"Do you?" the dominant pushed.

"No, sir."

The older man nodded, very slowly. "Good." He seemed to think for a few seconds, before he nodded once more, in the way that Devon was so familiar with. Mr. Templeton had made a decision. "The conversation is over, you needn't think about it again."

"Yes, sir," Devon whispered. It shouldn't have been as simple as that. A few words shouldn't have eased the pain, but the other man's acceptance of him wrapped around him, holding him just as tightly as Mr. Templeton gripped his wrist, and in a strange way, that did make it hurt less than it had before.

Their eyes met once more. Devon had seen that particular light in the older man's eyes a few times before, back at the office. It almost always meant that whatever happened next was going to instantly become one of his favourite memories ever.

"Please?" The word was out before he could stop it. The second it hit the air, he wanted to snatch it back.

He didn't ask. Whatever they did, it was the other man's decision. It was his job to obey orders, not to make requests. He didn't ask. Devon's eyes opened very wide. He scrambled to find the suitable words for an apology.

"Yes."

Devon blinked up at the older man, trying to fit the word into context.

"Yes," Mr. Templeton repeated, very calmly.

Not sure what else to do, Devon nodded his general agreement with the affirmative. A second later, with his hand still wrapped around Devon's wrist, the older man led him out of the kitchen.

Chapter Five

Two minutes later

Devon wasn't sure what he'd expected to be behind the door at the top of the stairs when Mr. Templeton unlocked it. Maybe a bedroom—an old fashioned and entirely masculine space that was filled to the brim with the dominant's personality as much as with his possessions. Dark wood. A neatly made bed. Everything arranged nicely and in its right place.

Reaching into the darkness of the room, Mr. Templeton clicked a switch. A light came on, illuminating the reality.

Old fashioned—maybe. Masculine—certainly. Kinky as hell—bingo!

Devon's gaze rushed from one item to another. First it fell on the neat rows of hooks on the far wall of the room, where an array of whips and floggers hung in perfectly organised lines. Next it went to the huge diagonal cross set up in the corner of the room, dark polished wood gleaming under the overhead light.

The sling in another corner caught Devon's attention for a moment, before the cage occupying another segment of the space called to him. Mr. Templeton stepped forward until he stood right in the middle of it all. And suddenly it was so easy to see him locking the door on that cage as Devon sat naked and vulnerable behind the bars.

The dominant folded his arms across his chest. It took no effort at all to imagine one of those big strong hands holding a whip. The breath caught in Devon's throat. His brain spun and screamed out for more oxygen, but it was too late—Devon's entire blood supply seemed to have been diverted directly to his cock.

"Do you remember the rules?" Mr. Templeton asked.

Devon pulled his attention to the other man's face as he took a step into the room. "I'm not saying no, sir. I don't want to leave." Another step forward. "We can do whatever you want."

Mr. Templeton stared down at him for several long moments. Devon forced himself to remain perfectly still as the dominant seemed to inspect his very soul.

Stepping closer, Mr. Templeton reached past him and pushed the door closed. It banged as it met the frame. Devon managed not to jump.

"You have free reign over the rest of the house, but you won't enter this room without my specific permission. Understand?"

"Yes, sir."

Mr. Templeton took a step back. "You have permission to look around."

Devon cautiously walked around the room, taking in every detail. Black leather, stainless steel, dark wood. He had to tighten his hands into fists at his sides to stop himself reaching out and caressing it all. He didn't have permission to touch, just to look. He didn't have permission to come, either, although he was pretty sure he could get off on nothing more than the sight and smell of his surroundings.

"Do you have any questions?" the dominant asked, eventually.

"Just one, sir," Devon said. His voice sounded strange to his own ears, slow and sleepy as if it were coming from a long way away.

As he turned to face the older man, Mr. Templeton nodded permission for him to ask it.

"What do you want to do first, sir?"

The older man's lips definitely twitched into a smile then. "Over time, you'll get to know every item in this room very well," he promised.

"Yes, sir." Devon wasn't sure what pushed more pleasure into his voice right then, the idea of playing with all the other man's toys, or the possibility that he might actually be kept around for long enough to do that.

"But there's no rush."

"Yes, sir," Devon repeated.

"Put your clothes on the bench."

The sheer familiarity of the order was a welcome beacon in the middle of a room that was far out of his range of experience. A command that he knew he was capable of completing to a standard that was likely to please his master soothed his soul.

Within a minute he stood in the middle of the room, his clothes folded neatly on the bench, and turned back to his master.

"Hold out your hands."

A few deft movements from his master, and Devon found both his wrists encircled by thick black leather cuffs. His ankles soon received the same treatment. The restraints were well padded, but they still fitted tightly around him, making sure he felt their presence with every second that passed.

His movements were his master's to permit or deny. He'd known that in the office, but he had never been so aware of the fact, nor quite so in love with it, as he was right then as he felt the leather embrace him for the first time.

"Come here."

Devon stepped forward, very conscious of the added weight around each limb. Mr. Templeton stood next to the heavy wooden beams that formed the diagonal cross. As he approached them, Devon spotted the ring hooks on the top and at the base of each length of polished mahogany.

Almost without needing to think about it, he offered up his wrists and ankles to be locked in place. His master stepped closer. Four metallic clicks echoed around the room. Devon's eyes fell closed. He sensed the larger man move away and he tensed against the cross, biting back a plea not to be left behind.

"No dominant who is worthy of the term walks away from a man on a whim, or just because someone else was stupid enough to doubt his worth." The words were spoken directly in front of him.

Devon's eyes snapped open. Mr. Templeton had moved to stand in the space between the cross and the wall. Devon looked up at him, staring helplessly into the older man's eyes.

"I told you that I own you whenever you're with me, didn't I?" his master asked.

"Yes, sir." The words were barely a whisper. The room seemed to absorb every ounce of false bravado out of them.

"But, sometimes a submissive needs more than words to remind him he is owned," Mr. Templeton went on.

"Sometimes a man needs to feel the leather against his skin holding him where he belongs, binding him to his master." Reaching up, he ran his fingers over the cuff around Devon's right wrist.

"Yes, sir."

The dominant could have said the sky was green and Devon would have made the same reply. Every word the older man said slid straight past that part of his brain that was worried about mere facts. They rushed to the instinctive bit of him that only cared about what the man in front of him was really talking about, really telling him.

"You're bound to me, Devon. And if you don't achieve the standard I expect of you, I'll see to it that you're trained and your behaviour improves until you do. But I won't walk away, and I won't send you away either."

Devon swallowed rapidly. "Yes, sir," he repeated.

As he stepped to the side of the cross, Mr. Templeton ran his fingers from the leather wrapped around Devon's wrist, down the outside of his arm and across his back. Even that chaste contact sent shockwaves racing through Devon's body. His cock curved up between the crossing lengths of wood towards his stomach.

"And sometimes a man needs to feel his master's touch *underneath* his skin in order to feel entirely safe in his master's possession of him."

"Yes, sir."

"That's very different to him deserving a punishment."

Devon had never heard the older man so serious about anything. "Yes, sir," he rushed out.

He sensed Mr. Templeton walking away from him then, but the sound of his footsteps on the hard, wooden floorboards soon heralded his return.

That was right, something inside Devon remembered. A dominant didn't walk away from his submissive — not in any way that really mattered.

Leather brushed across Devon's back. He looked over his shoulder. A flogger trailed over his skin, dozens of long black leather thongs caressing him with every tiny movement of his master's wrist.

Mr. Templeton stepped back once more. The leather left Devon's skin. It returned in a sweeping motion that struck his left shoulder and made its way down towards the right side of his waist, leaving a trail of heat in its wake.

He gasped, instinctively pulling at the cuffs.

No reprimand was issued for his lack of control, but Devon couldn't bring himself to look over his shoulder and see the other man's expression.

The flogger came down again, leaving another line of warmth from his right shoulder and to the other side of his waist. He stayed still. Pressing his lips together, he ensured no sound escaped.

A second passed and the leather kissed his skin again, no more harshly than it had the first time. Slowly it registered in Devon's mind that the pain he expected to flood into his veins wasn't there. He wasn't showing off his newly acquired self control skills by keeping back an agonised scream.

There was nothing to scream about. The warmth of the flogger's touch didn't really hurt as it seeped into his skin. It brought far more pleasure than pain.

The flogger kissed his back once more. Devon frowned slightly, as his brain tried to process the sensation and failed. His body had no choice but to deal with the flogger without his mind's help.

Trapped in the moment, with no idea when the leather would fall against him again, Devon found himself acutely conscious of every detail within his grasp, within his body.

His breaths began to speed up. His heart beat faster. As his muscles tensed, adrenaline pumped around his body more rapidly by the moment. Every time the flogger landed Devon rocked slightly in his restraints, but he had no idea if he was moving away from it or towards it.

It wasn't a punishment. Mr. Templeton had been very clear about that. It wasn't a punishment and his master wasn't angry with him. His master wanted to keep him around. Mr. Templeton wanted him to feel his master's touch beneath his skin and know he was owned.

Devon whimpered as his let his head fall forward. The heat was nothing like the fire that had burned in his buttocks when Mr. Templeton had spanked him. It was more a caress than a blow, more a kiss than a spank.

Biting down on his bottom lip, Devon tugged at his cuffs, searching for a sensation he could understand. The padding inside the leather made it impossible for him to hurt himself no matter how hard he pulled at them.

It was as if his master's hands were wrapped around his every limb, holding him safe and secure, keeping him exactly where he wanted him, protecting him from himself as much as from everything else in the world.

Nothing bad could happen. He couldn't let his master down right then. All he could do was stand there and take it as more and more unexpected pleasure seemed to race around his body.

His skin tingled and sung out under the lash. Heat spread through him. His cock gloried in every sensation. The tip rubbed against the crossing pieces of wood in front of him, teasing him, making him desperate to rise onto his toes and rub himself properly against the wood.

The flogger came down again. The sound of it against his skin filled the room. Devon released his bottom lip from his teeth. Unable to stay silent a moment longer, he tossed his head back and moaned his pleasure up to the ceiling.

Too much. Not enough. Unable to cope with what he'd already been granted, he still needed more—more of his master, and more of whatever else the dominant was willing to offer him too. He pulled more frantically at the cuffs as desperation swirled and writhed inside him.

As suddenly as the flogger had greeted him, its presence seemed to disappear from the world. Empty air was the only thing that brushed against his back. Every inch of skin from his shoulders to his buttocks purred its pleasure.

Devon arched and squirmed as if he might somehow be able to discover the flogger's location with his wriggling. A cool palm came to rest in the middle of his back. Devon gasped. He tried to look over his shoulder.

His master's other hand came to rest on the back of his head. Fingers stroked through his hair, gentling him down, holding him in place.

"Hush."

The hand resting on Devon's back stroked over his heated skin, tenderly caressing him and making his whole body ache with more pleasure than it knew how to process.

"That's right," Mr. Templeton said. More words followed. They flowed over Devon, not imparting any real information, merely telling him the other man was there and everything was fine.

Mr. Templeton stepped forward. His clothes brushed against Devon's back. His sensitised skin screamed out its joy.

The older man's arms slid around his torso, stroking across Devon's chest as they pulled him back tighter against his body. Mr. Templeton's clothes rubbed against his back, making him gasp and arch against him. His wrists pulled at the leather as he tried to get closer to his master.

"Good boy."

The larger man's hand slid down Devon's body, past the crossing lengths of wood, and wrapped around his erection. Devon whimpered. He pressed back against him all the more, glorying in an entire world full of sensations both above and beneath his skin.

Mr. Templeton's grip moved up and down around his cock, tightening and relaxing as pre-cum smeared against the dominant's palm and slicked Devon's shaft.

Balanced right on the edge, Devon clung to the tiny scrap of control he still possessed as he desperately tried to wait for permission.

"Come."

Devon had never been more grateful to hear a word hit the air. He stopped trying to hold back. A wave of pleasure so intense it felt far more like pain than the kiss of any flogger ever could coursed through him. He tossed back his head. A scream filled the air as he came into the other man's hand.

Mr. Templeton's grip around him never eased, never hesitated. He kept on stroking him again and again, as Devon's hips thrust forward as far as they were able and finally fell still.

Silence descended on the room. The only proof that a scream had ever filled the air was the rawness in Devon's throat. He whimpered as Mr. Templeton's hand kept moving long after he'd have asked for it to stop if that had been an option. But it wasn't even a possibility that night.

He couldn't have brought himself to refuse anything the other man was willing to offer him if his life had depended on it.

Finally, Mr. Templeton's hands fell away from him of their own volition. The cuffs disappeared a few seconds later, leaving Devon lost and all alone in the world, until Mr. Templeton's arm wrapped around him, steadying him as he stood naked in the centre of the playroom. His master turned Devon towards him, letting him lean against his body. A hand settled on the back of his head, encouraging him to rest his temple against the other man's shoulder, too.

"Hush."

The word seemed to seep under Devon's skin just as easily as the heat from the flogger had. It went straight to his heart and slowed the frantic beating.

Picking up his clothes as they passed the bench, Mr. Templeton carried them down the stairs as he led him from the room. Setting the garments neatly on the hallway table next to the phone, he walked Devon on into the living room.

With his head still spinning from adrenaline and afterglow, Devon's focus slowly began to return to him as he looked up at the older man.

Mr. Templeton smiled at him—a real, full smile. His knuckles brushed against Devon's cheek before he stepped back and put some distance between them.

Lacking an order to do anything else, Devon remained motionless where he'd been left as he watched the older man pick up a thick cushion and move it to rest on the floor at the base of an arm chair.

There was a table next to Devon. He rested his fingertips on the well polished surface as he sought for something to centre himself on. They brushed against something. He looked down. The book he'd brought in from the library.

"Come here, Devon. Bring your book with you."

His legs still more than a little unsteady, Devon followed the order. He crossed the room and settled himself on the cushion. Leaning back against the base of his master's chair, he found it was possible to lean his shoulder comfortably against the other man's leg and keep contact with him.

Devon looked down. His book rested on his lap. Desperate to please, he opened it and tried to read.

Mr. Templeton reached past him and gently closed it.

Devon glanced up at him, wondering if the other man was disappointed in him for being so fuzzy.

"There's no rush for that. Put it down. It'll still be there when you're ready for it."

"Yes, sir." The words were little more than a hoarse whisper.

Mr. Templeton turned away from him for a moment. He picked up something from beside his chair. A bottle of lemonade appeared in his hand as it came back into Devon's field of view.

The older man opened it and offered it to his submissive's lips.

It was only then that Devon realised how dry his throat was, how thirsty he was. He squirmed around and eagerly offered his lips up to the rim of the bottle. Just as Mr. Templeton was about to tip it up, Devon managed to see the world around him a little more clearly.

His gaze fell on the other man's crotch, where the fabric was disturbed by the line of his master's straining erection. Suddenly the lemonade wasn't important. He looked up to the other man's face. "May I—?"

Mr. Templeton shook his head. "This will do you more good at the moment."

Devon dropped his gaze.

"Later," the dominant promised. His fingers stroked through Devon's hair, pushing the messy blond strands back from his face.

"Yes, sir."

Devon offered his lips to the bottle again. The cool liquid slid down his throat, soothing the soreness his own cries had put there. A few moments passed. Mr. Templeton took the bottle away and set it aside.

Dropping his gaze, Devon wondered if later had arrived yet, if he'd be allowed to offer his master something in exchange for all the pleasure he'd given him, now.

Minutes ticked by slowly. Out of the corner of his eye he saw Mr. Templeton picking up his own volume. Leaning his head to one side, Devon let his temple fall against Mr Templeton's knee. A moment later, a hand settled in his hair and slowly stroked through the strands again.

The older man's words from earlier that day came back to the forefront of Devon's mind then. *When you don't have any orders or tasks you may rest.*

Devon's eyes fell closed and he did as he'd been told.

* * * *

Four hours later

Propping himself on one elbow, Andrew Templeton stared down at the younger man for several long seconds, wondering how the hell he'd managed to resist bringing the boy to his bed months before.

As he silently watched the submissive sleep, his hand tightened into a fist beneath the bedclothes. Even then, in the stillness and peace that had settled over the house as night fell, Devon's parents' opinions of their son repeated around and around inside his head. Forcing his fingers to relax, he reached out and stroked his knuckles down the sleeping boy's cheek.

If there was only one thing he did in the world, he knew in that moment, that it would be to do everything in his power to keep that kind of pain out of Devon's life.

It was a strange sensation. Protectiveness and possession, lust and something that might actually be a bit like love. After so long spent thinking of nothing but his own needs and desires, it was also faintly terrifying.

The submissive stirred. He leaned into his master's touch, half awake and half asleep. Gathering the smaller man closer to him and encouraging him to rest his head against his chest, Templeton dipped his head and pressed a chaste kiss to the top of the slumbering submissive's head.

After so long with no one to think of but himself, the realisation that he now had someone in his life who needed him just as much he might need them was going to take more than a little getting used to.

* * * *

Saturday 5th June 2010

As the twelfth chime rang out, Mr. Templeton rose from his chair and picked up his briefcase.

Devon knew what that meant. He tried not to grin like too much of an idiot at the idea of visiting the older man's house again. But, even if he couldn't quite keep the smile from his face, he still managed to walk out into the drive and slide into the passenger seat of his master's car with perfect composure. He was quite proud of that.

It was only when they'd been in the car for several minutes and driven some distance that Devon realised they weren't taking the same route as they had last time they'd driven away from the office.

Glancing at the other man out of the corner of his eye, Devon shifted slightly in his seat. He tried not to look nervous, tried not to show any doubts about whatever his master's decision turned out to be.

They would go wherever his master wanted them to go. They would do whatever Mr. Templeton wanted them to do when they got there. A good submissive knew that. A good submissive didn't doubt his master. Faith wasn't much for the older man to ask of him in return for everything he'd done for him since they met, and it wasn't even as if it would be *blind* faith. Mr. Templeton had never given him any reason to think he wasn't completely trustworthy.

Devon stared out through the windscreen for several seconds as he considered his options. Very slowly, his eyes fell closed. The world turned dark. Cautiously leaning his head back, Devon found the head rest and took a deep breath.

He didn't need to know where they were going. He didn't need to see where they were going either. That was his master's decision, his master's responsibility. All he had to do was trust, and follow his master's orders as he tagged along.

Within moments the submissive had lost track of the corners they'd turned. It didn't take much longer for him to lose all perspective of time. They could have been driving for minutes or hours. Devon still kept his eyes closed.

He didn't open them until the car stopped and the engine fell silent.

Devon blinked in the bright sunlight as he looked around. Tilting his head to one side, he looked up at the building Mr. Templeton had stopped alongside. He straightened his head, blinked, then looked again.

"I live there." He turned to his master.

The older man was half smiling again. "I'm aware of that. Go up to your flat and put some things in a bag to take to my house."

"Yes, sir." Devon opened the car door and stepped out onto the pavement. Being driven around with his eyes closed had to have addled his brain. There was no other reason why he'd want to turn back, peek into the car and say something like, "Would you like to come in, sir?"

Mr. Templeton regarded him in silence.

"I have coffee," Devon added. It was another bloody stupid thing to say. His master had to know that he had the right to go wherever the hell he wanted, and to drink anything he liked when he got there.

Devon stepped back, closed the door and turned towards the building, eager to follow the order, before he managed to keep the older man waiting for so long he'd decide to give up on him and drive away without him.

A sudden bleep behind him informed him a car had just been locked. Devon looked over his shoulder. Mr. Templeton walked around the car and joined him on his way into the building.

Unsure what to say as they rode up in the elevator, Devon studied their reflections in the mirrored doors.

It was as impossible as ever to try to work out what the other man was thinking from his expression. He didn't seem to be too annoyed. That was something to be grateful for at least. Devon pushed his hands deeper into his jeans pockets.

He was so lost in his thoughts and so busy cursing himself for his stupidity in inviting the other man in, he jumped as the lift jolted to a stop on the fifth floor.

The doors slid open. Devon stepped out into the hallway.

"It's this way, sir." He waved an arm to the right.

Mr. Templeton said nothing as he followed him down the corridor.

Devon walked more quickly, keen to reduce the time he had in which to make a fool of himself.

Unlocking the door to his flat, he stepped inside and quickly moved out of the small hallway to make room for his master.

Mr. Templeton followed him in and closed the door behind him. A few more paces were all it took for him to join Devon in what the marketing brochure had called the 'contemporary open plan layout'.

Devon let out a breath he hadn't realised he'd been holding, as he realised he'd remembered to put everything back in its rightful place before he left that morning. There were no dirty dishes left out. No clothes on the floor. No flaws for his master to pick him up on.

"I'll get that coffee, sir."

The kitchen wasn't much more than a corner of the other room. It was impossible for Devon to find any real privacy there in which to pull himself back together. All he could do was face the counter and take a deep breath.

Coffee.

He repeated the word to himself several times. Maybe if he just concentrated on that, he had a chance.

Taking his master's favourite blend from the cupboard above the counter, he carefully brewed up a mug, just as the other man liked it, and took it back into what passed for his living room.

"Thank you." Mr. Templeton smiled at him after he sipped it. "Very good."

A rush of relief mixed with pleasure at the compliment had a blush rushing to Devon's cheeks. He dipped his head in an effort to hide it.

"I should go pack that bag, sir," he muttered, turning away from him and quickly beating a retreat into the flat's only bedroom.

He was standing next to his bed, staring into an overnight bag without the damndest idea what his master expected him to put in it, when he heard a footfall behind him.

He remained exactly where he was as he sensed his master move closer.

"Devon?"

He froze as his master's hand came to rest on the small of his back. "Yes, sir?"

"If, for whatever reason, I took some insane dislike to your living arrangements, what do you think would happen?"

Devon continued to study his bag. "You'd tell me what I was doing wrong and how I could do better, sir?" he hazarded.

"Correct. And is that something you need to be afraid of?" His hand remained on Devon's back, the heat from his palm quickly soaking into his skin.

"No, sir."

"Good boy." Mr. Templeton's hand left him.

Devon sensed the older man walk back towards the bedroom door.

"Sir?" He spun around to face the other man. Mr. Templeton turned back towards him too.

"Is there anything in particular I should be packing?" Devon blurted out.

The dominant considered the question for a few seconds. "A few changes of clothes. A wash bag. Music. Books. Photographs. Whatever will make you feel at home."

"Yes, sir."

The other man nodded once, before he made his way back towards the living room.

Mr. Templeton wanted him to feel at home in his house. Devon felt that same pleased blush rush back to his cheeks. He smiled as he went back to his packing.

Minutes passed and he continued to put things in his bag, but as time went on, more and more of his attention strayed to wondering what his master might be doing in the adjoining room.

The moment the bag was full, Devon carried it into the living room. He found Mr. Templeton studying the beech shelves against the far wall.

"Did you choose these?" the older man asked. He sounded mildly impressed.

Devon shook his head as he ran his gaze over the artistically arranged pieces of abstract red glass and pottery. As much as he wished he could take credit for them, he couldn't bring himself to lie to his master. "I'm not good with things like that. There was a show home package thing. Pretty much everything came with the flat, sir."

He looked around the room then, as if seeing it for the first time. It was as blank and impersonal as Mr. Templeton's house was a complete representation of the older man's personality and taste.

Devon looked down, wondering what the older man must think of it, what he must think of a man who lived in such a soulless place.

It was neat and tidy, yes. But it could have belonged to any man on the planet who knew how to pick up after himself — any man who belonged to someone able to inspire him not to want live in the kind of mess the place had been before he'd first met Mr. Templeton.

"Is there something you wish to say?" Mr. Templeton asked him.

"No, sir," Devon whispered.

Even after he said that, the older man seemed to wait for him to say something else.

"I don't want to make excuses, sir."

"For what?"

Devon looked around the room. Right then he wished he had the balls to apologise for *everything*.

Mr. Templeton stepped forward and closed the gap between them. His fingers tucked under Devon's chin and encouraged him to look up.

The pain and the confusion in Devon's eyes tore at something in Templeton as their eyes met. Staring down at the smaller man, he wanted nothing more than to wrap his arms around him, pull him in close and tell him that everything would be well with the world for the rest of his life.

He stopped himself short before his new found inclination to soppiness took over completely.

"You have nothing to be ashamed of." He let the younger man see him turn his attention back to the room. His fingers stayed under Devon's chin, holding him in place, making sure the younger man's eyes remained on his master's face. "Nothing at all."

A little bit of assurance to give him the confidence to put more of a mark on his surroundings would obviously do him the world of good. But that would come with time. And it could hardly be considered the boy's fault anyway.

"I wish it was more like yours, sir."

Templeton stared down at the younger man in surprise. "In what way?"

"Your house is — it's exactly like you, sir."

Templeton let his fingers stroke up and down the younger man's throat as he thought about that.

"Yes, it is." He'd moulded it into something that was all about him over the last few years. Everything arranged just as he wanted it, with no allowances made for anything or anyone else.

"Did you pack your bag?" he asked.

"Yes, sir."

Templeton nodded his approval.

Having someone in his life whom he cared about enough to stop insisting on having *everything* his own way would no doubt do him the world of good too.

Chapter Six

Saturday 7th August 2010

Devon let out a breath he hadn't even realised he'd been holding as his master pushed open the door to the playroom and finally stepped inside it for the first time in what felt like forever.

Quickly approaching the doorway, Devon waited politely on the threshold for permission to enter too. It wasn't immediately granted. He stood there and watched as the older man made a slow circuit around the room, calmly running his gaze over all his toys and his options, as if only then deciding what he'd like to play with that day. Devon's heart raced even faster, as it occurred to him that he could be deciding *if* he wanted to play that day.

He had to want to play. He had to.

Devon did his best not to let his desperation show as he stared into the room and tracked his master's progress.

It had been weeks. It felt like years, but even according to the calendar, it had been weeks since the older man had invited him in there to play. He couldn't have come that far today, only to change his mind at the very last moment.

"Come here, Devon. Close the door behind you."

Already naked since they'd risen from his master's bed that morning, Devon shivered as the cooler air that always seemed to linger in the playroom caressed his skin. The blocked up window stopped the sun entering the space. It made sense that it should be chilly, but that wasn't the only reason why a shiver ran down Devon's spine.

He made no attempt to move his hands in front of him and hide how much he loved the idea of being in there again. His master was hardly likely to miss the fact he was ram-rod hard whatever he did.

Standing neatly in the middle of the room, he studied his master's body language very intently, trying to work out what he was thinking. Mr. Templeton had his back to him as he took something out of a cabinet. But still, Devon thought, he seemed…relaxed…almost peaceful in there?

When the older man turned back to him, he had a pair of very wide cuffs in his hands and a slight smile on his lips. He fitted the cuffs around Devon's wrists without a word. They extended up over his palms and the backs of his hands as far as his fingers. The thickness of the padding made it almost impossible for him to bend his wrists.

Unsure what was going to happen next, Devon couldn't even try to help as his master moved away to fetch whatever else he intended to involve in their latest scene.

When a low stool was placed in the middle of the room, a nod from his master finally let Devon know there was something he could do to please the older man. He rushed forward and stepped up onto it.

"Raise your hands."

The ceiling was high. His fingertips didn't come close to it. But the cuffs brushed against the chain hanging down from a fitting bolted to the plasterwork above his head as if it had been measured especially for someone of his exact frame and build.

With his extra height, Mr. Templeton didn't need to stand on anything to lock his submissive's cuffs to the chain.

Devon stared up at the padlock as it clicked into place and his master checked its hold on him by tugging firmly at the chain. Apparently satisfied, he took half a step back.

Something touched one of Devon's toes. He looked down. Mr. Templeton's shoe rested between his bare feet, right on the edge of the low wooden stool. The highly polished surface distorted slightly, as if the older man's foot was moving inside it.

The stool shifted beneath Devon. His eyes snapped up and focussed on his master's face. His throat instantly dry with nerves, he parted his lips, but no words emerged.

"Is there something you wish to say?" Mr. Templeton prompted.

Devon closed his mouth and shook his head.

"Something you want to ask?"

He shook his head again. He even managed to scrape up a verbal answer to go with the gesture. "No, sir."

As he held the dominant's gaze, Devon felt something slowly begin to settle inside him. There was no need to ask him anything. He trusted his master. Mr. Templeton had never let him down, and he wasn't going to start now.

The stool moved beneath his feet once more. Devon tensed, but he kept his eyes up and locked with his master's.

Another tiny movement of the stool, and suddenly it was gone. It disappeared from beneath his feet as Mr.

Templeton kicked it away. Devon's body dropped, just a fraction of an inch, as all his weight suddenly came to bear on his wrists.

Devon's legs automatically kicked out, desperately searching for any point of safety.

Mr. Templeton remained immediately in front of him. Pain shot through the submissive's toes as they kicked against something. Devon's eyes opened very wide as he realised he'd just struck his master, but his gaze never dropped.

His shoulders protested at the unfamiliar pressure on the joints, his heart raced so fast he was sure it couldn't manage to keep up with itself a moment longer, but somehow it did. And, very slowly, Devon began to scrape together some sort of self-control. He managed to still his legs. It was impossible to make his body instantly motionless. He swung gently as the momentum of his struggles slowly dissipated.

Silence fell over the room, to be disturbed by nothing other than Devon's gasping breaths.

"I'm sorry I kicked you, sir," he whispered.

Mr. Templeton shook his head, brushing the apology and the kick aside. "Hush."

Devon obediently hushed as the dominant's hand came to rest against his skin, just below his rib cage.

Every breath Devon dragged into his body pressed his diaphragm down against his master's hand. As Mr. Templeton stepped closer and stood to one side of him, he settled his other hand on Devon's back, steadying him, providing him with all the strength and security he could ever need.

Devon had no idea how long they remained there, neither of them moving, as his breaths slowly calmed and his heart ceased to race so frantically.

Although their bodies weren't touching, in the silent stillness, he became aware of his master's breaths and felt his body automatically try to follow them.

"That's right."

Devon closed his eyes as he relished the mild praise.

Just a second later, his master's hands left him.

He opened his eyes just in time to see Mr. Templeton leave his field of vision. Turning his head, Devon tried to look over his shoulder. His own arm was in the way. All he succeeding in doing was to set himself swinging all over again.

The dominant reappeared on the other side of him. His eyes ran over Devon's body, as it had so many times over the months, seeming to examine him for any flaws that might have appeared overnight. It was impossible not to squirm subtly under his assessment, and even the tiniest movement sent his whole body swaying and the chain above his head rattling, loudly relaying his weakness to his master.

Finally Mr. Templeton stepped forward. His fingertips trailed along Devon's cock, pulling a gasp from him. His hips instinctively tried to thrust forward and push his shaft into the older man's hand. The chains clanged. His cock still received nothing more than his master wished to bestow upon it.

A few more fingertip teases and he walked away again, out of the submissive's line of sight. Devon could almost have believed he was alone in the room, until slicked fingers slid against his buttocks.

He tried to part his legs and push out his arse in invitation. His movement couldn't have been symmetrical enough. He started to rotate slowly from his restraints making the room swirl around him. Trying to correct the movement only made it worse. Devon whimpered his frustration as he frantically tried to still himself, to turn himself back and regain his master's fingers.

Mr. Templeton didn't say anything. He just made him wait until he gently spun back into his original position and hung perfectly motionless before he gave his fingers back to the submissive. Devon held his breath, afraid that too much oxygen might start him spinning again.

He couldn't risk parting his legs as the dominant's fingers slid between his buttocks and worked their way inside his hole. Very slowly, they began to prepare him and work him open, sliding into his arse over and over again, deeper with each minute that passed.

Devon's breath escaped as a pleasure-filled moan as Mr. Templeton found his prostate. It was impossible for him to stay still then. He squirmed, trying to push back. The chains sang out as he began to sway. He lost his master's touch again.

He whimpered, closing his eyes to hide from his own weakness, mentally cursing himself for screwing up yet again.

Gradually, he realised something had changed within the room. Devon blinked his eyes open.

Mr. Templeton stood directly in front of him. His fly was undone, his hand wrapped around his condom covered shaft as he slicked it with extra lube. Devon's gaze dropped to watch, mesmerised by the other man's slow, rhythmical movements. His tongue flicked out to moisten his lips. A low moan escaped from the back of his throat as he realised there was no way in hell he'd be able to reach out to touch, to taste, to please his master in any way.

Eventually, he dragged his gaze back up to his master's face. He could keep the words back, but there was no way he could keep the pleading expression out of his eyes.

Mr. Templeton stepped forward. Reaching around him, he ran his hands down Devon's back. The submissive couldn't help but arch into the older man's touch then, but his master steadied him and stopped him swinging out of control.

There was still a trace of lube on one of his hands, slicking his fingers as his hand slid over Devon's arse. His master's hold on him slid down the backs of Devon's legs and pulled them up to wrap around the larger man's waist. The tip of Mr. Templeton's erection brushed against his hole as Devon squirmed and tried to get even closer to the other man with clumsy movements of his legs.

Devon bit his lip to keep his begging back, sure that his babbling would only annoy the older man. His master's face was right in front of him, his eyes as serious as ever as he guided Devon down onto his cock.

There was no way he could rush the dominant. All he'd ever succeed in doing if he tried was to lose what grip he had on him with his legs.

In tiny increments, Devon's master fed his cock into him. He gasped as the thick shaft stretched him open even further than the man's fingers had.

His teeth nipped at his bottom lip as he fought to adapt to the burning stretch more quickly. He met his master's eyes then. Even if he could hurry his own body along, he knew there was no way his master would be coaxed into quickening his pace.

Gradually, he relaxed and his body welcomed the other man inside him. As his head dropped back and pleasure filled him, Devon wriggled and managed to wrap his legs even more tightly around the other man's waist.

His master's hand palmed his arse, squeezing the tight, round muscles in his hands as he rocked his hips for the first time and buried his cock even further into Devon's arse.

Suddenly the burning ache in the submissive's shoulders didn't matter. The only things that he needed to think about were the pleasure rushing through him and his desperate attempts to try to offer some fraction of his joy back to the older man.

He tensed his muscles around the dominant's shaft again and again. Mr. Templeton moaned his appreciation as he rocked back and thrust into Devon once more. As he pulled his submissive closer, Devon's cock rubbed against the fabric of the older man's shirt, smearing pre-cum against the neatly ironed cotton.

Whimpering his pleasure, Devon tried his best to complement the rhythm his master set, but it was almost impossible for him to control his movements as he hung there. All the control rested with his master.

Suspended in mid air with the other man's cock deep inside him and his hands taking a tight grip on his body, Mr. Templeton became the only solid point of reference in Devon's world.

The cuffs around his wrists ceased to matter—the only thing that kept him safe and content and full of pleasure was the way his master held on to him.

"Sir…" That was the only word in his head.

He met his master's gaze just in time to see the pleasure rush through the older man's eyes as he jerked and ploughed his shaft in him to the hilt as he came, hard and fast. The dominant's hold on him tightened, his fingertips digging into Devon's flesh hard enough to leave marks that might even linger into the next day if the submissive was very lucky.

Gradually the older man's movements ceased, but Mr. Templeton still didn't break eye contact with Devon. Even as he stepped back and left him hanging there, the younger man's own erection still flourishing, curving back towards his stomach without any way of him to gain any friction against his aching shaft, Mr. Templeton held his gaze.

Turning his attention away for a moment, the dominant tidied up his clothes, disposing of the used condom and tucking his cock neatly away. That was all he needed to do to once more appear like the calm, collected businessman whom Devon had first met in the office so long ago.

Mr. Templeton hadn't changed at all. He'd just changed the man he owned beyond all recognition.

Devon closed his eyes and tried to gather together some kind of composure. He failed spectacularly, but a touch to his cheek informed him that his master wasn't angry with him.

Blinking his eyes open, Devon turned his face into his master's hand and kissed his palm. Mr. Templeton smiled at him then — one of those very rare real smiles that Devon had been lucky enough to receive from him over the last few weeks. Suddenly his own frustration didn't matter.

"Good boy."

Two words, one smile and everything was right with his world.

Templeton slowly took his hand away. As amazing as he looked strung up that way, it wouldn't do to leave him there too long — not on his first time, not when his joints weren't used to being put under that kind of tension.

Nudging the stool back under the submissive's feet, Templeton carefully undid the cuffs and guided the younger man to lower his arms.

A whimper escaped from the back of Devon's throat. His joints obviously didn't like that at all. His muscles appeared weak with submission as much as anything else.

And Templeton had no doubt that the younger man's head was going to be spinning from it all for some time yet.

Sliding one hand behind Devon's knees and the other around his body beneath his arms, he easily lifted him off the stool. The boy's eyes opened very wide as he turned to him, but his arms quickly settled themselves around his master's neck.

In spite of his surprise, the younger man made no complaint as Templeton carried him down the stairs and into the living room. Lowering himself into an armchair while Devon was still in his arms neatly placed the submissive on his lap.

The boy hesitated then, apparently not sure what to do with himself.

"That show you like is going to start soon." Templeton nodded to the remote laying well within the other man's reach.

Devon hesitated.

"Put it on."

He reached out and followed his master's order.

As the rather appalling show began to play, Devon slowly relaxed into his master's embrace. Templeton smiled over the top of his head as he blocked out the racket from the television and gave all his attention to the man in his arms.

There was a curious pleasure, not in having to do things for another person, but in choosing to do things for them anyway. In having all the control in the world, and using it to make someone whom he cared for happy.

Templeton brushed his knuckles against the submissive's erection, gently teasing him as the younger man curled into his master's embrace, more content than ever.

Saturday 1st January 2011

"Tell your master what's wrong."

Devon looked up from his desk as he heard the order.

Mr. Templeton stood in the doorway and stared back at him in silence for a full sixty seconds.

Devon still didn't know what to say at the end of the minute. He dropped his attention back to the book he had been staring at and not reading for the last half an hour.

"Devon?" the older man prompted.

"If I do something I shouldn't do, sir..." His courage failed him and he trailed off.

Mr. Templeton took a seat on the sofa closest to where Devon was, in theory at least, working on his latest evening class assignment. "Are you asking me if you'll be punished or if you'll be disowned?"

"Disowned, sir," he admitted.

"That won't happen." The older man sounded so sure of himself, so sure of everything.

Devon nodded. That being the case, there wasn't really any reason for him to hold back any longer. If the worst that could happen was a punishment, it was worth the risk.

Reaching into the backpack full of study texts, he took out a carefully wrapped package. Quickly closing the gap between them, he knelt down by his master's feet.

"My first wages came through and...and it's been a year since we first met, sir," he blurted out, offering the present up to him.

Mr. Templeton took the parcel from him and glared down at it as if he'd never seen such a thing before.

"I'm sorry. I shouldn't have." All at once that was obvious. Devon reached out to take it back and remove it from the other man's sight.

Mr. Templeton took it briskly out of his reach. He stared at it some more.

Devon gazed at it too. In hindsight the carefully tied ribbon had probably been a mistake. His master wasn't a ribbon sort of guy — even if it was a navy blue ribbon the same colour as the older man's favourite suit.

Very slowly the dominant turned the parcel over in his hands, before untying the ribbon and carefully undoing the silver wrapping paper, to reveal a small black box, about three inches square.

Devon held his breath as Mr. Templeton finally opened that box and moved the tissue paper aside.

Gold sparkled as he lifted the pocket watch from its hiding place and held it up to the light to be inspected.

It had been a stupid idea. Devon could see that now. It wasn't his place to give his master presents. And a silly timepiece was the worst possible thing he could have chosen to buy for the other man. As Devon stared up at the shining surface of the watch's case, all that was obvious.

His gaze moved to the wristwatch that Mr. Templeton always wore.

"You don't have to use it or anything, sir. I just thought—" A fingertip came to rest on Devon's lips, silencing him.

"It's a beautiful present, Devon. Thank you."

Relief rushed through the submissive. He hadn't screwed up.

When Mr. Templeton smiled at him, Devon smiled back. Dropping his gaze, he shuffled his knees slightly on the carpet, not quite sure what to do now that he'd put himself in that position.

"I should get started on dinner, sir."

Mr. Templeton didn't call him back when Devon rose to his feet and left the room.

Quickly making his way to the kitchen, the submissive carefully consulted the notes he'd made after the older man had taught him the spaghetti recipe the week before.

Having something to do with his hands helped put his mind at ease a little—it helped to reassure him that he had made progress in the last year. Twelve months ago he wouldn't have had a clue where to start. A year ago he'd probably have been drunk out of his mind at...

He looked at his wrist watch. Six o'clock on a Saturday evening. He shook his head. He still might not be worthy of the older man's attention, but at least he could take comfort in the fact that the man the dominant had turned him into was a damn sight better man than he'd been a year before.

* * * *

An hour later

Devon frowned as a light, musical ringing sound filled the air. He looked around the kitchen for the source of it. It didn't sound anything like the smoke alarm he'd set off a few weeks before, but his attention still went to the cooker first. It was only when he glanced across the kitchen table and his gaze fell on his master that he realised that the older man was the font of the sound.

Mr. Templeton didn't seem the least surprised. Reaching into his jeans, he took out his new pocket watch. Without the denim to muffle the sound, it sung out clearly as it chimed in the hour.

Devon blushed and turned his attention back to his spaghetti.

Mr. Templeton didn't say anything until they'd both finished their meal and all the dishes had been washed and put away.

Hesitating in the hallway, Devon silently prayed that he was going to be invited to the playroom, but the older man walked past that doorway without even glancing at it.

"Tomorrow."

Devon turned his head. His master was standing in the doorway leading into the living room, staring back at him.

"Sir?"

"We'll play tomorrow," the older man promised.

"Yes, sir."

* * * *

Sunday 2nd January 2010

"At the stroke of twelve on this day and on every day from now on, you will belong to me for twenty-four hours. Do you understand?"

"Yes, sir." Devon blinked at him. He ran through what his master had actually said. His mind went blank. "Pardon, sir?"

"At the stroke of twelve on this day and on every day from now on, you will belong to me for twenty-four hours." Mr. Templeton repeated, perfectly calmly.

Devon ran the numbers over in his head. He'd been getting good marks in his maths assignments, but he still double checked them. "That means all the time, sir," he hazarded.

"Yes, Devon. It does."

Looking up at his master, Devon nibbled on his bottom lip. His feet shuffled on the rug in front of the fireplace in

Mr. Templeton's living room as he tried to wrap his mind around the idea.

"All the time," he repeated, not so much asking a question as just needing to hear the words out loud again. "I'd belong to you all the time."

"Yes," Mr. Templeton said. "All the time."

Devon looked around the room as if he'd never seen it before, imagining how that would be. Mr. Templeton was half smiling at him when he looked back to his face, although there was also a touch of tension around his eyes that Devon had often seen when he first arrived at his master's side, but which rarely lingered there when they were together now.

"Leave your clothes on the table, and come sit with me." His master turned away from him then, and settled himself on the sofa opposite the fire.

The familiarity of the order gave Devon a concrete point of reference in a world that had suddenly shifted under his feet.

Quickly taking off the clothes he'd worn in Mr. Templeton's garden as he started to learn how to help him look after it, Devon crossed the room and knelt at his master's feet.

"Tell me what you're worried about."

"What if I screw up?" Devon blurted out. He was working his arse off and managing one hour of doing well each day, along with one full day on the weekends. The chances of that extending into twenty-four hours every day had to be so slim they'd be nonexistent.

"It's very possible you will," Mr. Templeton said. "And when that happens, we'll deal with it. I'll set out the rules I expect you to follow. If you break those rules, I'll expect you to accept the consequences — just as I do now."

"Yes, sir."

"How I'll treat you and what you can expect from me will remain exactly the same as it has always been, Devon. I'll look after you, and teach you, and do what I can to make sure you fulfil all your potential. But, it's important you understand that even if we're together for the rest of our lives, I'll still be your master, not your...your boyfriend, or anything else you might imagine."

Devon blinked at the other man. For just a moment, he tried to imagine Mr. Templeton as something other than exactly what the man he was. He shook his head at the possibility.

The atmosphere changed slightly. He sensed the strain in the older man double and re-double again.

"I wouldn't want you to be anyone other than you, sir," Devon rushed out.

Mr. Templeton offered him one brisk nod.

Devon dropped his gaze to the tiny patch of floor between them and tried to make his brain work.

Eventually Mr. Templeton tucked a knuckle under his chin and made him look up. "Is this what you want, Devon?" he asked, carefully studying his expression as if he wanted to search out any hint of doubt.

He wouldn't find any doubts. Devon met his master's gaze and held it. As quietly terrifying as the whole idea was, he didn't have any doubts about what his answer should be. If there was any chance of him getting exactly what he wanted from life, he had to take it.

"Yes, sir, I do want this—so much."

His master gave him just one simple nod in return. As easily as that, Devon had the distinct impression he'd given complete control of his body and possession of his soul to another man, to his master. It was done.

Adrenaline and endorphins rushed through him, making him light-headed. His mind span with pleasure.

He belonged to his master. No time limit, no cut off point. He belonged to his master. Full stop!

Devon had no idea what to do next. Instinct kicked in. He looked up at the older man in the hope that Mr. Templeton would tell him.

The dominant smiled and held out his hand. "Up here."

Devon cautiously rose from his knees and moved to the seat next to the older man.

"That's right," his master praised gently, guiding him to move closer and sit right next to him.

Devon glanced up. Their eyes met and suddenly Devon couldn't look away. He'd never quite grown used to being the centre of that sort of attention, and Mr. Templeton's focus upon him had never lessened over the months they'd spent together.

A knuckle came to rest under his chin to keep his head up. He remained perfectly still as his master leant forward and brought their lips together. Devon gasped as their mouths met for their very first kiss.

The older man's lips were strong against his. There was no hesitation as Mr. Templeton's tongue slid into his mouth and took instant possession of him. As they turned on the sofa, Devon reached up and settled his hands on the older man's shoulders to keep himself steady.

He whimpered as his master's tongue brushed against his. His fingers fisted against his master's shirt. The hand that had rested beneath his chin moved around behind his skull and threaded into his hair, holding his head back at the perfect angle as the dominant deepened the kiss.

Devon moaned his pleasure and tightened his grip on the other man's shoulders, savouring each moment. He bucked into his master's hand as fingers suddenly encircled his cock.

It had been so long since he'd been allowed to come, and he belonged to his master, and the dominant's tongue was laying claim to his mouth. He squirmed on the sofa, trying to stay still and simply accept his lover's touch, but finding himself entirely unable to do that. Within seconds he was close to coming. His hands clenched and unclenched against his master's shoulders as he tried to find some extra bit of self control that he hadn't been aware of possessing before.

Suddenly Mr. Templeton pulled away. Before Devon could scream out a protest, another word hit the air, one spoken by the other man.

"Come."

The word bypassed Devon's brain and went straight to his cock. By the time the dominant's lips returned to his, Devon was already spilling into the older man's hand. Some tiny part of his brain registered the sensation of cum falling on his bare skin and knew it had to be staining his master's clothes too. But far more of his brain was spiralling up through heights of pure bliss he hadn't even guessed at the existence of until that minute.

He gasped for breath as Mr. Templeton pulled back and looked down at him. It wasn't in him to resist or feign a kind of strength he didn't feel right then. When his master's hand guided him to lean forward and rest his head on the older man's shoulder, he was more than willing to do so.

He was vaguely aware of Mr. Templeton reaching past him for a wipe and cleaning his sticky hand, but the dominant didn't immediately order him back onto the floor and Devon had absolutely no intention of putting any extra distance between them until he was commanded to do so.

His master touched his cheek. Blinking open his eyes, Devon looked up at the other man. Then, of all the embarrassing things to do, he blushed.

Mr. Templeton chuckled and stroked his flushed cheek, guiding him to rest his face against his shoulder and lean into the solid strength of his body once more.

Minutes passed in silence. The submissive's brain started to work again. As much as he loved resting in his master's arms, Devon had to know, he had to speak up.

"Sir...?" As soon as he began, he trailed off, suddenly not sure if he really wanted to ask the question or not. It wouldn't do to let one kiss go to his head and make him think he could ask his master silly things whenever he felt like it.

"I've never been angry with you for asking a question, Devon. I'm not going to start now," his master promised, idly stroking his fingers up and down his back.

"Why me?" Devon blurted out. "That night in the club, sir. Why did you give the note to me and not someone else?"

"Because no one else in the bar was you," his master said very simply. "You have no idea how rare such a perfect submissive is, do you?"

Devon glanced at him. He might be a lot of things, but he knew damn well he wasn't perfect.

"As soon as I saw you, I knew you had the potential to be incredible if someone would only take the time and give you a little bit of direction. Without any sort of guidance, some submissives tend to drift rather aimlessly."

"That's what I was doing," Devon said, resting his head on his master's shoulder again, wrapping himself in the certainty his master provided for him.

"Yes," Mr. Templeton agreed. "A submissive without a master is almost as bad as a master without a submissive. Neither tends to do well without the other."

"You were doing well, sir," Devon corrected quickly.

His master pressed an unexpectedly tender kiss to the top of his head. "In some ways, perhaps. Dominants don't tend to become drifters as much as they become complete bastards. I don't think you know how much I've looked forward to noon over the last few months. Dominants need someone to look after, someone to love, just as much as everyone else."

A glance up at Mr. Templeton told Devon that he was perfectly serious. His master loved him. He parted his lips, the pent up declaration desperate to finally be allowed out. At the last moment he hesitated, not sure if he was allowed to say it.

Mr. Templeton just nodded his permission.

Devon swallowed. "I love you too, sir." They were barely a whisper, but they still made his master smile and brush their lips together once more.

At that moment, something broke the calm quiet. Devon's gaze dropped to his master's pocket as the kiss ended. The chimes finished their approach to one o'clock as the older man pulled out the watch and flicked open the case.

He hated the one o'clock chimes so much—almost as much as he'd grown to love the sound of the twelve o'clock chimes. Every muscle in his body tensed as he stared down at the gold and Mr. Templeton's fingers continued to stroke through his hair.

The short toll of one finished. The watch, and the whole world, fell silent.

"If you intend to try and hold your breath until noon tomorrow, you're going to make yourself very uncomfortable very quickly," Mr. Templeton whispered in his ear.

Devon looked up at his master. He let out a breath he hadn't realised he'd been holding. "I'm really allowed to stay, sir?"

Andrew Templeton smiled down at his submissive. "Yes, you are."

Devon blinked at him. He nibbled at his bottom lip.

"If you want something, ask," Templeton prompted, when it became obvious no words would be spoken if he didn't.

"A few more minutes here, sir?" Devon asked, very softly, as he looked at where they sat together on the sofa.

Templeton nodded. "Just a few then."

He quickly settled his head on his master's shoulder as if that was all he could ever want to do for the rest of his life. Templeton gathered him closer into his arms and only half pretended he was doing that entirely for his submissive's benefit.

Devon's cheek moved against Templeton's shoulder as the younger man smiled to himself. Templeton smiled over the top of his head too.

A year to the day. Whatever the submissive's less than sober recollections might be, it was a year ago in the very early hours of that morning that he'd finally given in to the temptation to approach the boy. And now the submissive finally belonged to his master — for twenty-four hours, from the stroke of twelve on that day and on every day to come.

About the Author

Kim Dare is a twenty-seven year old full time writer from Wales (UK). First published in December 2008, Kim has since released over thirty BDSM erotic romances.

While the stories range over male/male, male/female and all kinds of ménage relationships and have included vampires, time travellers, shape-shifters and fairytale re-tellings, they all have three things in common—kink, love and a happy ending.

Kim loves to hear from readers. You can find her contact information, website details and author profile page at http://www.total-e-bound.com.

Total-E-Bound Publishing

www.total-e-bound.com

Take a look at our exciting range of literagasmic™
erotic romance titles and discover pure quality
at Total-E-Bound.

8773038R0

Made in the USA
Lexington, KY
01 March 2011